BUFFY
THE VAMPIRE SLAYER™
"Once More, With Feeling"

BUFFY
THE VAMPIRE SLAYER™

"Once More, With Feeling"

SIMON PULSE

NEW YORK LONDON TORONTO SYDNEY SINGAPORE

All interviews and additional materials courtesy of Paul Ruditis

Historian's Note: This teleplay represents the original shooting script for the episode "Once More, With Feeling"; thus we have preserved all typos and mis-attributions. The script may include dialogue or even full scenes that were not in the final broadcast version of the show because they were cut due to length. Also, there may be elements in the broadcast that were added at a later date.

First Simon Pulse edition December 2002

™ and © 2002 by Twentieth Century Fox Film Corporation. All Rights Reserved.

SIMON PULSE
An imprint of Simon & Schuster
Children's Publishing Division
1230 Avenue of the Americas
New York, NY 10020

Editor: Micol Ostow
Editorial Team: Lisa A. Clancy and Lisa Gribbin
Video grabs provided by Omni Graphics
Designed by *Lili Schwartz*
The text of this book was set in Trade Gothic Condensed.

Printed in the United States of America
10 9 8 7 6 5 4

ISBN 0-689-85918-X

Library of Congress Control Number 2002110676

Acknowledgements

Special thanks to the cast and crew of Buffy the Vampire Slayer, especially Joss Whedon, Marti Noxon, David Fury, Christophe Beck, Cynthia Bergstrom, Robert Hall, Joel Harlow, Todd McIntosh, Carey Meyer, Adam Shankman, Ray Stella, Jesse Tobias, Christopher Buchanan, Michael Boretz, and Kern Eccles. We'd also like to thank Greg Curtis at Fox Music.

And with much gratitude to everyone at the Simon & Schuster Children's Division, including Russell Gordon, Lauren Ackerman, Efraim Salzberg, Steve Brezenoff, Ellen Krieger, Kristina Peterson, Alan Smagler, Nellie Kurtzman, O'Lanso Gabbidon, and Lauren Edelstein. Thanks also to Debbie Olshan at Twentieth Century Fox, without whom this book would be little more than a gleam in our eye.

We gratefully, finally, acknowledge Elizabeth Shiflett for her original proposal.

Table of Contents

Introduction

They said it couldn't be done.

They said it was too much, too expensive and difficult. That it would never come together—that I'd be laughed at. So, sadly, I put aside my plan to build a giant robot that eats hemorroids, and wrote some dinky musical instead. This is a book about it.

Yes, gentle reader, this is your chance to gently read all about the trials and triumphs of one of the finest hours (and eight minutes) of television ever to air on that particular night. Read here about the laughs, the tears, the weird rash that I'm pretty sure Nicky gave me. The disastrous out of town opening, the hilarious fights between the composer and the librettist, the aging dancer who didn't think he could dance with a snooty ballerina . . . I'm sorry, that was *The Bandwagon*. Totally different. I'm very tired.

What you will find in this book, apart from the script, music, and lyrics of the most difficult piece I have ever tried to write, is a truly detailed and absorbing look behind the process, lovingly compiled and then bound with a cover like a book would be. I wrote "Once More, With Feeling" knowing I had every chance in the world of falling on my face, of making a show that would make America long for the halcyon days of *Cop Rock*. What gave me the confidence to go ahead anyway was beer. Beer, megalomania, and most of all the knowledge that I was surrounded by such talented folk that anything I could turn out that was even adequate, they could make extraordinary. I mean my cast, of course, but also the crew, the arrangers—all the people interviewed within. It's gratifying for me to read about them: the Production Designer, the D.P., Wardrobe—to hear their view of the process and to make a comparative chart showing who didn't praise me enough. (They'll be hearing from some of my other, deadlier robots fairly soon.)

The same attention to detail and affection for the material is shown by the folk who compiled this book. And I'm grateful for it, because I loved this show. I love musicals, and whether mine is forgotten in thirty seconds or remembered for minutes to come, I'm proud to have made one.

Well, enough introductionizing. The book is yours—the world of our little musical drama unfolds to you by a simple yet revolutionary new "page-turning" process. Enjoy!

I said, enjoy.

I'm not kidding. You better. I'll know.

—*Joss Whedon*

Preface

"Going Through the Motions"
PREVIOUSLY ON *BUFFY THE VAMPIRE SLAYER* . . .

The emotional admissions made by the Scooby gang while under the spell of the musical demon known as Sweet came from secrets and story lines built from considerable development. Each character had his or her own hidden feelings that grew out of the complex storytelling woven by Joss Whedon and the writing staff over the five previous seasons.

Giving up her own life to save that of her "newfound" sister, Buffy dove through a dimensional portal opened by the evil being known as Glory and sacrificed her life to save not only Dawn, but the world one last time. Her friends then took her place as protectors of Sunnydale under the watchful eye of Giles and the grow-

ing magickal powers of Willow. Once the team of slayerettes had proven their mettle in battle, Giles felt that he could finally leave the town in their capable hands. He went home to England melancholic and blaming his own failures for the death of his Slayer. However, unbeknownst to the former Watcher, the gang, led by an even more powerful Willow than anyone suspected, had plans to bring the Slayer back to life.

As Willow prepared herself for the ritual revival, it became more and more obvious that she was toying with very dark magic. It was an unnatural progression from her early dabblings in the craft when Giles had warned her against powers that she was not strong enough to control. Now she was becoming a powerful witch, but the question began to arise of whether she was controlling the magic or it was controlling her. Her girlfriend, Tara, was the first to see how the power was beginning to overtake Willow.

The revival spell worked and the Slayer was reborn. Though shaken, Buffy began to live her life with her friends again as they congratulated themselves for saving her from a hell dimension in which they had naturally assumed she had been trapped. In the celebrations that followed, Xander and Anya finally announced their engagement, which they had been keeping secret at Xander's request. Xander had told Anya that he wanted to keep the engagement quiet during the tumult surrounding Buffy's return, never admitting that the real reason for his silence was his own doubts. But now he was ready to share his joy with his friends.

Dawn was overjoyed to see her sister return, but almost immediately fell back into the confused role of a neglected child. Since their mother's death Dawn and Buffy had been pulling away from each other, unsure of the new dynamics of their relationship. Dawn's rebelliousness had more recently manifested itself in her stealing items from the Magic Box and other stores around town as a silent plea for attention.

Once notified that his Slayer was back, Giles returned from England cautiously pleased to see Buffy alive again. He knew that she was going to have to readjust to her life and take on the role of an adult, but felt that he was standing in the way. With him around as a father figure, he knew that Buffy would never grow into the guardian that Dawn needed her sister to be. Not willing to abandon his charge right away, Giles could not admit to her that his return from England was only temporary.

Spike, who was always a peripheral member of the gang, was also overjoyed by Buffy's return. The vampire had experienced growing and entirely unrequited feelings for the Slayer over the past year. Although she would not return his love, Buffy still felt a connection to Spike as he was the only one to whom she would admit that her friends had not saved her from Hell, but stolen her from Heaven.

"Once More, With Feeling"

Episode # 6ABB07
Story # E01429

BUFFY THE VAMPIRE SLAYER

"Once More, With Feeling"

Written and Directed By

Joss Whedon

SHOOTING DRAFT

September 18, 2001(WHITE)
September 20, 2001 (BLUE)
September 21, 2001 (PINK)

BUFFY THE VAMPIRE SLAYER

"Once More, With Feeling"

<u>CAST LIST</u>

BUFFY SUMMERS........................ Sarah Michelle Gellar
XANDER HARRIS........................ Nicholas Brendon
RUPERT GILES......................... Anthony S. Head
WILLOW ROSENBERG..................... Alyson Hannigan
SPIKE................................ James Marsters
ANYA................................. Emma Caulfield
TARA................................. Amber Benson
DAWN................................. Michelle Trachtenberg

SWEET................................ Hinton Battle   *
DEMON................................ Zachary Woodlee   *
HANDSOME YOUNG VICTIM MAN............ Daniel Weaver   *
MAN.................................. David Fury
YOUNG WOMAN.......................... Marti Noxon   *
HENCHMAN............................. Scot Zeller   *

BUFFY THE VAMPIRE SLAYER

"Once More, With Feeling"

SET LIST

INTERIORS

BUFFY'S HOUSE
    BUFFY'S BEDROOM
    UPSTAIRS
    WILLOW AND TARA'S BEDROOM
    DAWN'S BEDROOM
THE MAGIC BOX
    TRAINING ROOM
XANDER'S APARTMENT
    BEDROOM
    LIVING ROOM
SPIKE'S CRYPT
GRAVE
THE BRONZE

EXTERIORS

GRAVEYARD
STREET OUTSIDE THE MAGIC BOX
PARK
ALLEY
STREET
ALLEY BEHIND THE MAGIC BOX
VARIOUS STREETS
OUTSIDE THE BRONZE

BUFFY THE VAMPIRE SLAYER

TEASER

There is NO TEASER. There is a previously, and then the main
title. Time permitting, we might have a Chris Beck
Orchestral version of the theme and do old fashioned hero
shots, where the actors just smile or look glamorous over
their credits. Or we might not. Anyhoo, no teaser, so on
with it then.

END OF TEASER

ACT ONE

There will be an OVERTURE that runs the length of the opening
credits. We see various wordless scenes of scooby life that
all contain the common thread of Buffy going through her day
with a singular lack of involvement. Though people may
speak, we will not hear dialogue. We start with the episode
title:

ONCE MORE, WITH FEELING

And as it fades out we tilt down to see an old fashioned
alarm clock ringing, shaking about. (Probably the only noise
we'll hear.) It's set for 7:00. Widen to see

1 INT. BUFFY'S BEDROOM - MORNING   1

Buffy. Lying in bed, just looking at the clock. She takes
it, looks at it -- never bothering to turn it off.

2 INT. UPSTAIRS SUMMERS HOUSE - MORNING   2

We Brumman about the upstairs as the girls go about their
morning routine. Start on the hall as Buffy comes slowly out
of her room, headed for the bathroom -- but Dawn races in
before her, slamming the door. Buffy just stands there -- as
Willow, already dressed, comes briskly from downstairs to
grab some books from the bedroom. We see Tara in there,
making the bed -- Willow kisses her on the cheek as she exits.

Tara moves her pillow to find a small weed-like flower under
her pillow. She looks at it, puzzled, then smells it and
smiles, interpreting it as a romantic gesture. She is
twirling it in her fingers as she enters the bathroom,
opening the door to find Dawn just finishing brushing her
teeth. Tara moves to leave but Dawn indicates come in, she's
just leaving, she races out, Buffy still waiting in the
hall - and Tara shuts the bathroom door in Buffy's face,
never even seeing her. A beat, and Buffy turns and goes back
into her room, crawls back into bed.

3 INT. THE MAGIC BOX - AFTERNOON   3

Much movement in here as well -- customers mill about as
Giles takes an item from Dawn, reshelving it and giving her
a stern look.

Anya is looking at a bridal magazine, Xander, Willow and Tara
are in research mode. Willow and Tara make notes, while
Buffy also writes intently in a loose-leaf pad.

CONTINUED

3 CONTINUED: 3

   Come around to see that she has colored the entire page
   black, and is just filling in the last little bit.

   Giles appears in front of her with a serious looking axe and
   a hopeful smile. Buffy smiles back -- politely, and gets up,
   pulling off her outer shirt or sweater to reveal training
   clothes beneath. As they enter the training room, we go up
   to see a clock above it saying 4:30.

4 EXT. GRAVEYARD - NIGHT   4

   Buffy walks through the unusually blue night, looking around
   her as the overture finishes and she begins to sing:

                    BUFFY
              EVERY SINGLE NIGHT
              THE SAME ARRANGEMENT
              I GO OUT AND FIGHT THE FIGHT
              STILL I ALWAYS FEEL
              THIS STRANGE ESTRANGEMENT
              NOTHING HERE IS REAL
              NOTHING HERE IS RIGHT
              I'VE BEEN MAKING SHOWS OF TRADING
              BLOWS
              JUST HOPING NO ONE KNOWS
              THAT I'VE BEEN

   She is attacked by a vamp, and fights with him in a rote (and
   unusually synchronized) style --

                    BUFFY (cont'd)
              GOING THROUGH THE MOTIONS
              WALKING THROUGH THE PART
              NOTHING SEEMS TO PENETRATE MY HEART

   -- this last as she stake the vamp in the heart.

   He dusts as she moves on, finding two more VAMPS and a DEMON
   who is ritualistically sacrificing a HANDSOME YOUNG VICTIM
   MAN who is tied to a tree.

                    BUFFY (cont'd)
              I WAS ALWAYS BRAVE
              AND KIND OF RIGHTEOUS
              NOW I FIND I'M WAVERING
              CRAWL OUT OF YOUR GRAVE
              YOU FIND THIS FIGHT JUST
              DOESN'T MEAN A THING

   -- socking a vamp, whose head whips toward camera --

                                                            CONTINUED

4 CONTINUED: 4

                         VAMP 1
                    SHE AIN'T GOT THAT SWING

-- He drives his elbow back into her face, sending her flying
back to the ground.

                         BUFFY
                    THANKS FOR NOTICING

As she's getting up, the two vamps and the Demon march into
frame, singing. As they continue, she kicks up, grabs the
demon's sword and kills a vamp (off screen), knocking the
other down then stabbing the demon fatally --

                    DEMON AND VAMPS
               SHE DOES PRETTY WELL WITH FIENDS FROM
               HELL
               BUT LATELY WE CAN TELL
               THAT SHE'S JUST
               GOING THROUGH THE MOTIONS
               FAKING IT SOMEHOW

                         DEMON
               SHE'S NOT EVEN HALF THE GIRL SHE --
               OW...

He drops dead, as Buffy cuts the young man loose without even
looking at him. We see now that he is handsome indeed.

                         BUFFY
               WILL I STAY THIS WAY FOREVER
               SLEEPWALK THROUGH MY LIFE'S ENDEAVOR

                    HANDSOME YOUNG VICTIM MAN
               HOW CAN I REPAY --

                         BUFFY
               -- WHATEVER
                    (moving off)
               I DON'T WANT TO BE
               GOING THROUGH THE MOTIONS
               LOSING ALL MY DRIVE

The last vamp picks himself up and comes for her, getting
staked pretty quickly --

                    BUFFY (cont'd)
               I CAN'T EVEN SEE IF THIS IS REALLY ME
               AND I JUST WANT TO BE

Close on the vamp as he dusts, revealing Buffy's close-up:

                                                    CONTINUED

4 CONTINUED: (2)   4

                              BUFFY (cont'd)
              ALIVE

A long shot arms up away from her, the handsome young victim
man walking away unnoticed, the vampire's dust swirling past
camera in the breeze as the last note rings out and we cut to

THE BELL in the door of

5 INT. THE MAGIC BOX - DAY   5

As Buffy enters to find the gang (minus Dawn and Spike)
gathered about. Giles and Anya are going over her ledgers,
Tara and Willow off in the corner stocking jars. They're
very touchy and giggly, basking in each other this morning.
(Tara and Willow, not the other two.) Xander sits at the
table with a bunch of pastries, choosing one.

                    GILES
              Good morning, Buffy.

                    WILLOW
              Dawn get off to school all right?·
              She made the bus this time?

                    BUFFY
              What? Oh. I think so.

                    TARA
              I left her lunch in the fridge.
              Brown paper bag that said 'Dawn' on
              it. And also said 'lunch'.

                    BUFFY
              Then she probably took it when she
              probably got on the bus.

She crosses to the seated Xander, drops her bag on the table.

Xander plays with food, holding a long glazed cruller and a
powdered donut. The cruller speaks:

                    XANDER
              "Respect the cruller. And tame the
              donut!"

                    ANYA
                    (not looking up, not
                     meaning it)
              That's still funny, sweetie.

                                                    CONTINUED

5 CONTINUED: 5

Buffy, still standing, tries to broach a subject she's not
entirely comfortable with.

                    BUFFY
          So, uh... no research? Nothing going
          on? Monsters, or whatnot?

General murmurs of no, not really, not so much...

                    BUFFY (cont'd)
          Good. Good. That's uh... so, did
          anybody, um... last night, did
          anybody, oh... burst into song?

Everybody stops. The couples exchange looks.

                    XANDER
          Merciful Zeus.

          WILLOW   GILES
     (looks at Tara)   Well, I sang, but I have
     We thought we were the only my guitar at the hotel and
     ones! It was bizarre!   I often...

                    TARA
          We were talking, and
          then... It was like...

                    BUFFY
          Like you were in a musical?

                    GILES
          ...of course that would explain the
          huge backing orchestra I couldn't see
          and the synchronized dancing from the
          room service chaps...

                    ANYA
          Xander and I were fighting about
          Monkey Trouble.

                    BUFFY
          You have monkey trouble?

                    XANDER
             (unenthused)
          It's a film.

                    ANYA
          It's a corker!

                    XANDER
          Especially the ninth time.

                                              CONTINUED

5 CONTINUED: (2)   5

                          ANYA
              And we were arguing and then
              everything rhymed, and there were
              harmonies and a dance with coconuts...

                          XANDER
              It was very disturbing.

                          GILES
                    (to Buffy)
              What did you sing about?

                          BUFFY
              I, uh... I don't remember. But it
              seemed perfectly normal.

                          XANDER
              But disturbing. And not the natural
              order of things and do you think
              it'll happen again? 'Cause I'm for
              the natural order of things.

They are gathering around at this point.

                          GILES
              We should look into it.

                          WILLOW
              Exactly. With the books, and
              mulling, there could be mulling...

                          TARA
              Do we have any books about this?

                          XANDER
              Well, we've just gotta break it down,
              look at the factors, before it
              happens again --

                          GILES
              I'VE GOT A THEORY
              THAT IT'S A DEMON
              A DANCING DEMON -- NYEHH, SOMETHING
              ISN'T RIGHT THERE

                          WILLOW
              I'VE GOT A THEORY
              SOME KID IS DREAMIN'
              AND WE'RE ALL STUCK INSIDE HIS CRAZY
              BROADWAY NIGHTMARE

                                                        CONTINUED

5 CONTINUED: (3)   5

                         XANDER
              I'VE GOT A THEORY WE SHOULD WORK THIS
              OUT

                         WILLOW/ANYA/TARA
              I'S GETTING EERIE
              WHAT'S THIS CHEERY SINGING ALL ABOUT

Xander stands, urgent.

                         XANDER
              IT COULD BE WITCHES
              SOME EVIL WITCHES

-- As he turns to see Willow and Tara glaring at him --

                         XANDER (cont'd)
                    (sheepishly)
              WHICH IS RIDICULOUS 'CAUSE WITCHES
              THEY WERE PERSECUTED WICCA GOOD AND
              LOVE THE EARTH AND WOMAN POWER
              I'LL BE OVER HERE

                         ANYA
              I'VE GOT A THEORY
              IT COULD BE BUNNIES

ANGLE: EVERYBODY ELSE.

Stares at Anya. There is the sound of crickets.

                         TARA
              I'VE GOT A --

Anya interrupts with a heavy metal wail, the orchestration
backing her changing just as abruptly.

                         ANYA
              BUNNIES AREN'T JUST CUTE LIKE
              EVERYBODY SUPPOSES
              THEY GOT THEM HOPPY LEGS AND TWITCHY
              LITTLE NOSES
              AND WHAT'S WITH ALL THE CARROTS
              WHAT DO THEY NEED SUCH GOOD EYESIGHT
              FOR ANYWAY
              BUNNIES, BUNNIES
              IT MUST BE BUNNIES

Slight beat. The music returns to the previous sound.

                         ANYA (cont'd)
              OR MAYBE MIDGETS

                                              CONTINUED

5 CONTINUED: (4)   5

                              WILLOW
                        ("she's insane")
                  I'VE GOT A THEORY WE SHOULD WORK THIS
                  FAST

                              GILES/WILLOW
                        ("yup")
                  BECAUSE IT CLEARLY COULD GET SERIOUS
                  BEFORE IT'S PASSED

                              BUFFY
                  I'VE GOT A THEORY
                  IT DOESN'T MATTER

Giles looks up at this, perturbed. But Buffy takes the song,
explaining:

                              BUFFY (cont'd)
                  WHAT CAN'T WE FACE IF WE'RE TOGETHER
                  WHAT'S IN THIS PLACE THAT WE CAN'T
                  WEATHER
                  APOCALYPSE
                  WE'VE ALL BEEN THERE
                  THE SAME OLD TRIPS
                  WHY SHOULD WE CARE

The group joins in, not getting the undercurrent.

                              GROUP
                  WHAT CAN'T WE DO IF WE GET IN IT
                  WE'LL WORK IT THROUGH WITHIN A MINUTE
                  WE HAVE TO TRY
                  WE KNOW WE'LL PAY THE PRICE
                  IT'S DO OR DIE

                              BUFFY
                  HEY, I'VE DIED TWICE

She gives a wry smile to Giles, who is won over and joins in,
singing over the group.

                              GROUP
                  WHAT CAN'T WE FACE IF WE'RE TOGETHER

                              GILES
                  -- WHAT CAN'T WE FACE

                              GROUP
                  WHAT'S IN THIS PLACE THAT WE CAN'T
                  WEATHER

                              GILES
                  -- IF WE'RE TOGETHER

                                                        CONTINUED

5   CONTINUED: (5)   5

                              GROUP
                    THERE'S NOTHING WE CAN'T FACE

                              ANYA
                    EXCEPT FOR BUNNIES...

The number is over. There is a long pause.

                              XANDER
                    See okay that was disturbing.

                              WILLOW
                    I thought it was neat.

                              BUFFY
                    So what is it? What's causing it?

                              GILES
                    Thought it didn't matter.

                              BUFFY
                    Well I'm not exactly quaking in my
                    stylish yet affordable boots but
                    there's definitely something
                    unnatural going on. And that doesn't
                    usually lead to hugs and puppies.

                              ANYA
                    Well, is it just us? Is it only
                    happening to us? That would probably
                    mean a spell, or...

A beat. Buffy goes to the front door, opens it.

6   EXT. STREET OUTSIDE THE MAGIC BOX - CONTINUING   6

We see a big smiling close up of a MAN as the camera pulls
back and up -- it's the end of a huge production number. The
man is holding a dry-cleaned shirt still on the hanger and in
plastic.

                              MAN
                    THEY GOT THE MUSTARD OUT

Behind him, others fan out similar shirts of varying colors,
a few finishing dance moves in the background -- and Buffy
herself, very tiny in the corner of the frame, watching.

                              CHORUS
                    THEY GOT THE MUSTARD OUT!

7   INT. THE MAGIC BOX - CONTINUING   7

      Buffy shuts the door.

                          BUFFY
                It's not just us.

8   INT. THE MAGIC BOX - AFTERNOON   8

      The bell rings again as Dawn enters, excited. The group is
      at the books. Willow and Tara are still in their own love
      bubble. Buffy's not working that hard.

                          DAWN
                Oh my god you will never believe what
                happened at school today.

                          BUFFY
                     (not looking up)
                Everybody started singing and dancing?

                          DAWN
                     (glaring)
                I gave birth to a pterodactyl.

                          ANYA
                Oh my god! Did it sing?

      Deflated, Dawn joins them.

                          DAWN
                So, you guys too, huh?

      As they talk, Dawn wanders over to the counter, where a
      beautiful small TALISMAN on a chain is sitting, almost hidden
      away by other junk.

                          XANDER
                So, what'd you sing about?

                          DAWN
                     (enthusiasm gone)
                Math.

      She pockets the talisman, unseen.

      Willow is whispering in Tara's ear with a wicked smile. Tara
      suppresses her own, puts on serious face as she says:

                          TARA
                That's right! The, the volume! The
                text!

                                                    CONTINUED

8   CONTINUED: 8

                    GILES
          What text?

                    WILLOW
          The volumey... text.

                    TARA
          You know.

                    WILLOW
          The... murnenfurm report.

                    XANDER
          The what now?

                    TARA
          We just have a few volumes at the
          house that deal with mystical chants,
          bacchanals... might be relevant.

                    WILLOW
          We could...

                    GILES
          Well, I'm a hair's breadth from
          investigating bunnies at this point,
          so I'm open to anything.

                    WILLOW
          We'll check it out, we'll give you a
          call.

                    TARA
          Yeah, this could blow the whole thing
          wide open.

9   EXT. PARK - AFTERNOON   9

     Willow and Tara head for the house, taking a scenic shortcut
     beneath some trees.

                    TARA
          Do we have any books at all at home?

                    WILLOW
          Well, who wants to stay cooped up on
          a day like this? The sun is shining,
          there's songs going on, those guys
          are checking you out...

                    TARA
          What?

                                              CONTINUED

9 CONTINUED: 9

In fact, a couple of good looking college types are giving
Tara the once over as they pass at a bit of a distance.

                    TARA (cont'd)
          What are they looking at?

                    WILLOW
          The hotness of you, doofus.

                    TARA
          Those boys thought I was hot?

                    WILLOW
          Entirely.

                    TARA
          Oh my god. I'm cured! I want the
          boys!

She starts feebly after them, Willow grabbing her arm and
spinning her back to her.

                    WILLOW
          Do I have to fight to keep you?
          'Cause I'm not large with the butch.

                    TARA
          I'm just not used to that. They were
          really looking at me.

                    WILLOW
              (smiling)
          And you can't imagine what they see
          in you.

                    TARA
          I know exactly what they see in me.
          You.
              (sings)
          I LIVED MY LIFE IN SHADOW
          NEVER THE SUN ON MY FACE
          IT DIDN'T SEEM SO SAD, THOUGH
          I FIGURED THAT WAS MY PLACE

She walks into a pool of sunlight, looking around her.

                    TARA (cont'd)
          NOW I'M BATHED IN LIGHT
          SOMETHING JUST ISN'T RIGHT
              (turning to Willow)
          AM I UNDER YOUR SPELL
          HOW ELSE CAN IT BE
              (more)

                                                          CONTINUED

9 CONTINUED: (2)   9

                         TARA (cont'd)
               ANYONE WOULD NOTICE ME
               IT'S MAGIC I CAN TELL
               HOW YOU SET ME FREE
               BROUGHT ME OUT SO EASILY

She takes Willow by the hand and they walk, moving in sync;
flowing, dancing movement as they make their way through the
park.

                         TARA (cont'd)
               I SAW A WORLD ENCHANTED
               SPIRITS AND CHARMS IN THE AIR

She traces her hand through the air, leaving a fairy-dust
trail of light.

                         TARA (cont'd)
               I ALWAYS TOOK FOR GRANTED
               I WAS THE ONLY ONE THERE

Willow does the same -- and her light trail is more
spectacular still.

                         TARA (cont'd)
               BUT YOUR POWER SHONE
               BRIGHTER THAN ANY I'VE KNOWN
               AM I UNDER YOUR SPELL
               NOTHING I CAN DO
               YOU JUST TOOK MY SOUL WITH YOU
               YOU WORKED YOUR CHARM SO WELL
               FINALLY I KNEW
               EVERYTHING I DREAMED WAS TRUE
               YOU MAKE ME BELIEVE

Willow takes her, spins her -- and we are suddenly in

10 INT. WILLOW AND TARA'S BEDROOM - AFTERNOON   10

As they are still spinning, slowing, settling on the bed,
coming close to each other, close enough to kiss...

                         TARA
               THE MOON TO THE TIDE
               I CAN FEEL YOU INSIDE
               AM I UNDER YOUR SPELL
               SURGING LIKE THE SEA
               PULLED TO YOU SO HELPLESSLY

Tara throws herself back onto the heap of pillows. We stay
close on her as Willow moves over her, then back out of
frame...

                                                    CONTINUED

10 CONTINUED: 10

                    TARA (cont'd)
          I BREAK WITH EVERY SWELL
          LOST IN ECSTASY
          SPREAD BENEATH MY WILLOW TREE

     And we are still tight on her as she rises slowly from the
     bed, up into midair, floating...

                    TARA (cont'd)
          YOU MAKE ME COMPLETE
          YOU MAKE ME COMPLETE
          YOU MAKE ME COMPLETE

                                              SMASH CUT TO:

11 INT. THE MAGIC BOX - AFTERNOON   11

     The music cuts off abruptly as we see Xander say:

                    XANDER
          I bet they're not even working.

                    BUFFY
          Who now?

                    XANDER
          Willow and Tara. You see the way
          they were with each other? The get-a-
          roominess of them. I'll bet
          they're --
               (seeing Dawn)
          -- singing. They're probably singing
          right now.

                    GILES
          I'm sure Willow and Tara are making
          every effort.

                    XANDER
          Oh yeah.

                    BUFFY
          Xander...

                    DAWN
          It's okay, Buffy. I do know about
          this stuff. Mom and I had the
          singing talk a year ago. Besides, it
          is all kind of romantic.

                    XANDER/BUFFY
          No it's not.

                                              CONTINUED

11 CONTINUED: 11

                          DAWN
        Come on, songs, dancing around...
        what's gonna be wrong with that?

                                        SMASH CUT TO:

12 EXT. ALLEY - NIGHT   12

A man is dancing, a frenetic little tapdance that he clearly
has been doing for hours -- he is sweaty and panicking, but,
Red Shoe-like (the ballet not the diaries), he can't stop.
He is breathing heavily, like he's going to have a heart
attack -- but still with the fake smile on his face, selling
it.

He continues dancing. He begins to smoke.

And IGNITES, spontaneously burning down to ash and bone
remnant.

As his burning corpse falls, we see a pair of feet standing
by it. Arm up behind a figure, a man nattily dressed in a
retro kind of a suit, almost a zoot suit, coming up behind
his head to see that he is no man at all. Definitely demon,
though we see almost nothing of his face in the darkness.

No one knows his name, but we will call him SWEET. He looks
down at the smoking corpse, smiles.

                        SWEET
        That's entertainment...

                                   BLACK OUT.

                END OF ACT ONE

ACT TWO

13 INT. XANDER AND ANYA'S BEDROOM - MORNING   13

They are just sitting up from waking. Their jammies have a
forties retro feel to them -- her with the sexy little slip
(or shorts and camisole), him with silk jammies that actually
match. He tries to rub the sleep from his eyes.

                    XANDER
          You want some breakfast, baby?

                    ANYA
          You don't have to get to work?

                    XANDER
          I shut the crew down for the day. My
          guys start dancing around, I don't
          think I could deal. It's a flab
          thing. So. Waffles?

                    ANYA
              (affectionately)
          Will you still make me waffles when
          we're married?

                    XANDER
          No I'll only make them for myself,
          but by California law you will own
          half of them.

They kiss.

                    XANDER (cont'd)
          Or I can do an omelette -- you know
          I've almost got that pan flipping
          thing down, there was just that
          one... incident, and the fire
          marshall was much less --

As he continues, Anya gazes at him affectionately, his voice
fades out as she turns and ADDRESSES THE CAMERA as she sings

                    ANYA
          THIS IS THE MAN THAT I PLAN TO
          ENTANGLE -- ISN'T HE FINE
          MY CLAIM TO FAME WAS TO MAIM
          AND TO MANGLE -- VENGEANCE WAS MINE
          BUT I'M OUT OF THE BIZ
          THE NAME I MADE I'LL TRADE FOR HIS
          THE ONLY TROUBLE IS...
          I'LL NEVER TELL.

                                        CONTINUED

13 CONTINUED: 13

Now she starts talking -- but we don't hear 'cause Xander
begins, also looking (sometimes) at the camera.

                    XANDER
          SHE IS THE ONE, SHE'S SUCH WONDERFUL
          FUN
          SUCH PASSION AND GRACE
          WARM IN THE NIGHT WHEN I'M RIGHT
          IN HER TIGHT
                    (catches himself)
                         -- EMBRACE, TIGHT EMBRACE

He embraces her enthusiastically. She wriggles out of his
grasp, standing as he continues...

                    XANDER (cont'd)
          I'LL NEVER LET HER GO
          THE LOVE WE'VE KNOWN CAN ONLY GROW
          THERE'S JUST ONE THING THAT -- NO
          I'LL NEVER TELL

                    XANDER/ANYA
          'CAUSE THERE'S NOTHING TO TELL

That last note is entirely discordant. They ignore it, not
saying anything, moving into

14 INT. XANDER AND ANYA'S LIVING ROOM - CONTINUING   14

They go about their business, Xander heading for the kitchen
while Anya retrieves and flips through the paper.

                    ANYA
          HE SNORES

                    XANDER
          SHE WHEEZES

                    ANYA
          SAY 'HOUSEWORK' AND HE FREEZES

                    XANDER
          SHE EATS THESE SKEEZY CHEESES
          THAT I CAN'T DESCRIBE

He pulls one from the fridge, displaying a green moldy horror.

                    ANYA
          I TALK -- HE BREEZES

                    XANDER
          SHE DOESN'T KNOW WHAT 'PLEASE' IS

                                                    CONTINUED

14 CONTINUED: 14

                         ANYA
              HIS PENIS GOT DISEASES
              FROM A CHUMASH TRIBE

                      XANDER/ANYA
              THE VIBE
              GETS KIND OF SCARY

                         XANDER
              LIKE SHE THINKS I'M ORDINARY

                         ANYA
              LIKE IT'S ALL JUST TEMPORARY

                         XANDER
              LIKE HER TOES ARE KIND OF HAIRY

                      XANDER/ANYA
              BUT IT'S ALL VERY WELL
              'CAUSE GOD KNOWS I'LL NEVER TELL

                         ANYA
              WHEN THINGS GET ROUGH HE
              JUST HIDES BEHIND HIS BUFFY
              NOW LOOK -- HE'S GETTING HUFFY
              'CAUSE HE KNOWS THAT I KNOW

                         XANDER
              SHE CLINGS -- SHE'S NEEDY
              SHE'S ALSO REALLY GREEDY
              SHE NEVER --

                         ANYA
                    (interrupting)
                    -- HIS EYES ARE BEADY!

                         XANDER
              THIS IS MY VERSE, HELLO
              SHE --

But Anya starts dancing excitedly to attract attention so he
can't criticize her any further.

                         ANYA
              Look at me! I'm dancin' crazy!

She continues, Xander stares at her with deadpan contempt --
and then joins in, the two of them in perfect sync with the
crazy dancin'.

As the music continues, he sweeps her into his arms and they
do a few turns, getting closer and closer.. the resentment
melting away...

                                                    CONTINUED

14 CONTINUED: (2)   14

                    XANDER/ANYA
          YOU KNOW

                    XANDER
          YOU'RE QUITE THE CHARMER

                    ANYA
          MY KNIGHT IN ARMOR

                    XANDER
               (looking her over)
          YOU'RE THE CUTEST OF THE SCOOBIES
          WITH YOUR LIPS AS RED AS RUBIES
          AND YOUR FIRM YET SUPPLE -- TIGHT
          EMBRACE...

He instigates another dance break. Again, this one goes from
frenetic to romantic, as the two of them settle down on
either side of the table, looking at each other.

                    ANYA
          HE'S SWELL

                    XANDER
          SHE'S SWELLER

                    ANYA
          HE'LL ALWAYS BE MY FELLER

                    XANDER
          THAT'S WHY I'LL NEVER TELL HER
          THAT I'M PETRIFIED

                    ANYA
          I'VE READ THIS TALE
          THERE'S WEDDING THEN BETRAYAL
          I KNOW THAT COME THE DAY I'LL
          WANT TO RUN AND HIDE

They get up, coming closer to each other.

                    XANDER/ANYA
          I LIED
          I SAID IT'S EASY
          I'VE TRIED
          BUT THERE'S THESE FEARS I CAN'T QUELL

                    XANDER
          IS SHE LOOKING FOR A POT OF GOLD

                    ANYA
          WILL I LOOK GOOD WHEN I'VE GOTTEN OLD

                                              CONTINUED

14 CONTINUED: (3)   14

                        XANDER
              WILL OUR LIVES BECOME TOO STRESSFUL
              IF I'M NEVER THAT SUCCESSFUL

                        ANYA
              WHEN I GET SO WORN AND WRINKLY
              THAT I LOOK LIKE DAVID BRINKLEY

                        XANDER
              AM I CRAZY

                        ANYA
              AM I DREAMIN'

                        XANDER
              AM I MARRYING A DEMON

                        XANDER/ANYA
              WE COULD REALLY RAISE THE BEAM IN
              MAKING MARRIAGE A HELL
              SO THANK GOD I'LL NEVER TELL
              I SWEAR THAT I'LL NEVER TELL

                        XANDER
              MY LIPS ARE SEALED

                        ANYA
              I TAKE THE FIFTH

                        XANDER
                   (waving the camera
                    away)
              NOTHING TO SEE
              MOVE IT ALONG

                        XANDER/ANYA
              I'LL NEVER TELL

They collapse onto the sofa, laughing in classic post-musical
number style.

                                        SMASH CUT TO:

15 EXT. STREET - DAY   15

                        XANDER
              It's a nightmare. It's a plague!

                        ANYA
              It has to be stopped, Rupert --

                                                        CONTINUED

15 CONTINUED: 15

                    XANDER
          It's like a nightmare about a
          plague --

They are walking with Giles, their attitudes in sharp
contrast to what we saw in the living room. They are
frantically pissed, talking over each other.

          XANDER   ANYA
It was just like, I didn't I felt like we were being
wanna be saying things but watched, like a wall was
they just kept pouring out missing from our apartment,
of me and they rhymed and   like there only three
they were mean and   walls, no forth wall and
     (at Anya)   (at Xander)
My eyes are not beady!   **My toes are not hairy!**

                    XANDER
          Giles, you gotta` stop it.

                    GILES
          Well, I am following a few leads,
          and --

                    ANYA
          Plus, our number was clearly a retro
          pastiche that's never gonna be a
          breakaway pop hit.

                    XANDER
          Work with me, british man. Give me
          an axe and show me where to point it.

                    GILES
          As ever, it's not quite that simple.
          But I have learned something quite
          disturbing...

We don't hear what it is though Giles talks on, for as they
talk they pass a number in progress: a YOUNG WOMAN trying to
sing her way out of a parking ticket. The cop writes on,
unimpressed as she pleads:

                    YOUNG WOMAN
          NO...
          IT ISN'T RIGHT, IT ISN'T FAIR
          THERE WAS NO PARKING ANYWHERE
          I THINK THAT HYDRANT WASN'T THERE

She keeps singing, but the sound fades as we hear our gang
again, having passed her...

                                        CONTINUED

15 CONTINUED: (2)   15

                    XANDER
          As in, burnt up? Somebody set people
          on fire? That's nuts!

                    ANYA
          I don't know. One more verse of our
          little dittie I woulda been lookin'
          for the gas can...

                    GILES
          Certainly emotions are running high,
          but as far as I could tell the
          victims burnt up from the inside.
          Spontaneously combusted. I just saw
          the one -- I managed to examine the
          body while the police were taking
          witness arias.

Three janitors with brooms dance cheerily by in the
background. Our gang pays them no heed.

                    XANDER
          But we're sure the two things are
          related? Singing and dancing and
          burning and dying?

                    GILES
          We're not sure of much. Buffy's
          looking for leads in the local demon
          haunts... at least, in theory she is.
          She doesn't seem to...

                    XANDER
          She's easing back in. We brought her
          back from an untold hell dimension,
          remember? Ergo, weirdness. The
          important thing is that you're there
          for her.

They stop, Giles quietly confiding in Xander.

                    GILES
          I'm helping her as much as I can,
          but...

                                        DISSOLVE TO:

16 INT. SPIKE'S CRYPT - EVENING   16

The last rays of the sun are fading out as Buffy enters
Spike's crypt. He's coming up the ladder as she shuts the
door behind her. She has her usual lack of urgency.

                                        CONTINUED

16 CONTINUED: 16

                    SPIKE
          The sun sets, and she appears. Come
          to serenade me?

                    BUFFY
          So you know what's going on.

                    SPIKE
          Well, I've seen some damn funny
          things, last two days. Six hundred
          pound Chorago demon making like Yma
          Sumac, that one'll stay with you. I
          remain immune, happy to say. Drink?

                    BUFFY
          A world of no. You know anything
          about what's causing this?

                    SPIKE
              (a little bitter)
          So that's all, then. Just want to
          pump me for information.

                    BUFFY
          What else would I want to pump you
          for? I really said that, didn't I?

                    SPIKE
          Yeah, well, I won't bore you with the
          small talk. Don't know a thing.

Buffy senses the tension in him.

                    BUFFY
          What's up? You're all bad moody.

                    SPIKE
          S'nothing. I'm glad you could stop
          by.
              (off her look)
          It's nothing.

                    BUFFY
          What.

                    SPIKE
              (sings)
          I DIED

He's as startled as she by the fact that he just sang two
words. Is he really gonna...?

                                              CONTINUED

16 CONTINUED: (2)   16

                          SPIKE (cont'd)
          SO MANY YEARS AGO
                    (speaks:)
          Bloody hell...
                    (sings:)
          AND YOU CAN MAKE ME FEEL
          LIKE IT ISN'T SO
          BUT WHY YOU COME TO BE WITH ME
          I THINK I FINALLY KNOW

He gives himself over to it, rounding on her as he continues:

                          SPIKE (cont'd)
          YOU'RE SCARED
          ASHAMED OF WHAT YOU FEEL
          AND YOU CAN'T TELL THE ONES YOU LOVE
          YOU KNOW THEY COULDN'T DEAL
          BUT WHISPER IN A DEAD MAN'S EAR
          THAT DOESN'T MAKE IT REAL

The music gets a little harder now, some rockosity...

                          SPIKE (cont'd)
          THAT'S GREAT
          BUT I DON'T WANNA PLAY
          'CAUSE BEING NEAR YOU TOUCHES ME
          MORE THAN I CAN SAY
          AND SINCE I'M ONLY DEAD TO YOU
          I'M SAYING STAY AWAY
          AND LET ME REST IN PEACE

He flops onto the stone slab of the tomb as he sings the
final phrase. Buffy is thrown by the request. But Spike is
back up in a heartbeat, jumping off the tomb and circling her

                          SPIKE (cont'd)
          LET ME REST IN PEACE
          LET ME GET SOME SLEEP
          LET ME TAKE MY LOVE AND BURY IT
          IN A HOLE SIX FOOT DEEP
          I CAN LAY MY BODY DOWN
          BUT I CAN'T FIND MY SWEET RELEASE
          SO LET ME REST IN PEACE

He drops to his knees in front of her, defiantly supplicant.
And awfully close.

                          SPIKE (cont'd)
          YOU KNOW
          YOU'VE GOT A WILLING SLAVE
          AND YOU JUST LOVE TO PLAY THE THOUGHT
                    (more)

CONTINUED

16 CONTINUED: (3)   16

                          SPIKE (cont'd)
              THAT YOU MIGHT MISBEHAVE
                    (back up in her face)
              BUT TIL YOU DO I'M TELLING YOU
              STOP VISITING MY GRAVE
              AND LET ME REST IN PEACE

He throws the door open with this last.

17 EXT. GRAVEYARD - NIGHT   17

ANGLE ON: A FUNERAL PROCESSION

We see six men carrying a coffin toward an open grave where
the priest and mourners wait. They are walking solemnly in
time with the suddenly soft music.

Spike sings as we see angles of the proceedings, and he is
revealed walking with Buffy by the event.

                          SPIKE
              I KNOW I SHOULD GO
              BUT I FOLLOW YOU LIKE A MAN POSSESSED
              THERE'S A TRAITOR HERE BENEATH MY
              BREAST
              AND IT HURTS ME MORE THAN YOU'VE EVER
              GUESSED
              IF MY HEART COULD BEAT IT WOULD BREAK
              MY CHEST
              BUT I CAN SEE YOU'RE UNIMPRESSED
              SO LEAVE ME BE LET ME REST IN PEACE

He turns and jumps off a tombstone right onto the coffin the
men are carrying. As the chorus continues, he throws himself
flat on the coffin just as the lead men drop it and he back
somersaults right into the midst of the mourners, frightening
them all away by morphing into vampface as he sings:

                          SPIKE (cont'd)
              LET ME GET SOME SLEEP
              LET ME TAKE MY LOVE AND BURY IT
              IN A HOLE SIX FOOT DEEP
              I CAN LAY MY BODY DOWN
              BUT I CAN'T FIND MY SWEET RELEASE

At this point Buffy roughly grabs him away, he de-morphs and
they spin, stumble and they both go tumbling into the grave.

18   INT. GRAVE - CONTINUING   18

She lands on top of him, aware of the closeness as he
finishes:

                    SPIKE
          SO LET ME REST IN PEACE
          WHY WONT YOU
          LET ME REST IN PEACE

A moment of that old charged sexuality, and Buffy pushes
herself up --

19   EXT. GRAVEYARD - CONTINUING   19

-- pushes so hard the she comes flying out of the grave and
lands on her feet, takes off running.

The mourners have mostly gone as Spike sticks his head out of
the grave, looks with a forlorn, hesitant expression at the
retreating Slayer.

                    SPIKE
          So... you're not staying, then?

20   INT. DAWN'S BEDROOM - NIGHT   20

Dawn is dumping her bookbag contents on the bed as Tara pokes
her head in.

                    TARA
          Lotta homework?

                    DAWN
          Math. It seemed so cool when we were
          singing about it...

                    TARA
          Well, Willow said they got a lead on
          this whole musical extravaganza evil.
          This Demon that can be summoned, some
          Lord of the Dance -- but not the
          scary one. Just a demon.

                    DAWN
          Do they know who summoned it?

                    TARA
          They don't even know its name yet.
          But Willow'll find out. She's the
          brainy type.

                                                    CONTINUED

20 CONTINUED: 20

                    DAWN
          I'm glad you guys made up.

                    TARA
          What?

                    DAWN
          That whole fight you guys had about
          magic and stuff. It gives me belly
          rumblin's when you guys fight.

                    TARA
          Dawn, we never talked about...

                    DAWN
          It's okay, I mean I can handle it.
          It's just, you guys are so great
          together, I just hate it when -- but
          that was like the only real fight
          I've seen you guys have anyway. But
          I'm still glad it's over.

As Dawn is saying this, a horrible notion crosses Tara's
mind. She pulls the little flowery herb from her pocket,
looks at it.

                    TARA
          Dawn, I... there's something I need
          at the shop. Will you be okay for a
          little while?

                    DAWN
          Yes, the fifteen year old can spend
          half an hour alone in her locked
          house.

                    TARA
              (already leaving)
          I won't be long...

She's gone. Dawn's face falls slightly. A beat, and she
pulls the necklace she swiped from the magic shop from her
pocket and slowly puts it on, looking in the mirror.

                    DAWN
              (sings)
          DOES ANYBODY EVEN NOTICE

She opens a drawer -- there are a bunch of clearly pilfered
items in there.

                    DAWN (cont'd)
          DOES ANYBODY EVEN CARE --

                                                    CONTINUED

20 CONTINUED: (2)   20

She turns and **SCREAMS** at the **horrible PUPPET HENCHMAN** before her. Before she can move, two more surround her and throw a burlap sack over her head.

                              BLACK OUT.

                         END OF ACT TWO

ACT THREE

21 INT. BRONZE - NIGHT   21

We are close on Dawn as she awakens, no longer in a sack.
She lifts her head up, looks around and discovers that she is
on the pool table at the Bronze, light, streaming down
dramatically on her.

She starts to move -- and there is a deliberateness to her
movement that lets us know even before she hits the floor
that this is a dance. (Well, there's music, too. That
helps.) Dawn dances almost classically, her gestures just
slightly exaggerating her very real distress.

She takes a few quick looks about her, then rushes for the
door. It is locked.

She heads for another exit -- and a henchman appears, also
dancing. Forcing her back. She turns and faces the second.
They box her toward the middle of the dance floor. She
spins, then drops dramatically backwards, caught one foot
from the floor by the third henchman. He hoist her back up,
she turns, all three of them coming for her...

One grabs her arm and spins her around, throwing her towards
the stage, she goes down on her knees and slides, ends up
right in front of a staircase coming down from the middle of
the stage, her head at eye-level with a pair of very natty
shoes.

That begin to tap.

He taps his way down the staircase and as Dawn rises and
backs away from him (the henchmen retreating into corners),
we get a look first at his bright blue suit, then for the
first time, his face. Pure grinning evil, but not a bad
looking guy. A monster with style.

                    SWEET
          WHY'D YOU RUN AWAY
          DON'T YOU LIKE MY STYLE?

On the last word he stamps his foot and his suit instantly
changes color to bright burnished red.

                    SWEET
          WHY DON'T YOU COME AND PLAY
          I GUARANTEE A GREAT BIG SMILE

And here he literally tears the smile off his face And holds
it out to her. it begins to sing the next line before it
disappears and we whip back to see it's on his face again.

                                              CONTINUED

21 CONTINUED: 21

                         SWEET
             I COME FROM THE IMAGINATION
             AND I'M HERE STRICTLY BY YOUR
             INVOCATION
                     (unraveling a
                     parchment that looks
                     like an invitation)
             SO WHAT'D YOU SAY
             WHY DON'T WE DANCE A WHILE

He does dance about her a bit as he continues. She doesn't
join in, but her posture clearly shows she is still in the
mode...

                         SWEET
             I'M THE HEART OF SWING
             I'M THE TWIST AND SHOUT
             WHEN YOU GOTTA SING
             WHEN YOU GOTTA LET IT OUT
             YOU CALL ME AND I COME A-RUNNIN'
             I TURN THE MUSIC ON -- I BRING THE
             FUN IN
             NOW WE'RE PARTYING -- THAT'S WHAT
             IT'S ALL ABOUT
             I KNOW WHAT YOU FEEL, GIRL
             I KNOW JUST WHAT YOU FEEL, GIRL

He sways with Dawn, who finds herself somewhat drawn in by
his power...

                         DAWN
             So, you're, like... a good demon?

His laugh is as charming as it is unsettling.

                         DAWN (cont'd)
             Bringing... the fun in...

                         SWEET
             WHEN THESE MELODIES
             THEY GO ON TOO LONG
             ALL THAT ENERGY
             WELL IT COMES ON WAY TOO STRONG
             ALL THOSE HEARTS LAID OPEN - THAT
             MUST STING
             PLUS SOME CUSTOMERS JUST START
             COMBUSTING

He opens a conveniently placed door to let a smoking corpse
fall at Dawn's feet.

                                              CONTINUED

21 CONTINUED: (2)   21

                         SWEET
               THAT'S THE PENALTY
               WHEN LIFE IS BUT A SONG

He rounds on her now, all sweet menace

                         SWEET
               YOU BROUGHT ME DOWN AND DOOMED THIS
               TOWN
               SO WHEN WE BLOW THIS SCENE
               BACK WE'LL GO TO MY KINGDOM BELOW
               AND YOU WILL BE MY QUEEN

She's, well, a little thrown.

                         SWEET
               'CAUSE I KNOW WHAT YOU FEEL, GIRL

                         DAWN
               NO YOU SEE
               YOU AND ME
               WOULDN'T BE VERY REGAL

                         SWEET
               AND I MAKE IT REAL, GIRL

                         DAWN
               WHAT I MEAN
               I'M FIFTEEN
               SO THIS 'QUEEN' THING'S ILLEGAL

But he's into his routine, not paying her much heed as he
dances...

                         SWEET
               I CAN BRING WHOLE CITIES TO RUIN
               AND STILL HAVE TIME TO GET A SOFT
               SHOE IN

                         DAWN
               NO THAT'S GREAT
               BUT I'M LATE
               AND I'D HATE TO DELAY HER

                         SWEET
               SOMETHING'S COOKING - I'M AT THE
               GRIDDLE
               I BOUGHT NERO HIS VERY FIRST FIDDLE

                         DAWN
               SHE'LL GET PISSED
               IF I'M MISSED
               SEE, MY SISTER'S THE SLAYER

                                              CONTINUED

21 CONTINUED: (3)   21

He stops cold. Turns to her.

                    SWEET
          The Slayer?

                    DAWN
                (nervous)
          Yuh huh.

Sweet whips his head around to his henchmen.

                    SWEET
          Find her. Tell her... tell her
          everything. Just get her here. I
          want to see the Slayer burn.
                (sings)
          NOW WE'RE PARTYING
          THAT'S WHAT IT'S ALL ABOUT

22 INT. MAGIC BOX - TRAINING ROOM - NIGHT   22

     Buffy kicks a wooden plank in two. Giles is holding it.

                    GILES
          Good. Good.

                    BUFFY
          Am I supposed to bow now, or... have
          honor or something?

                    GILES
          It may seem hokey, but we need to
          work on precision and concentration
          as much as power. We're still not
          sure what we're facing.

                    BUFFY
          You'll figure it out. I'm just
          worried this whole session is going
          to turn into a training montage from
          an eighties movie.

                    GILES
          Well, if we hear any inspirational
          power chords we'll just lie down
          until they go away. Anyway, I don't
          think we need to work too much on
          strength.

                    BUFFY
          Yeah, I'm pretty spry for a corpse.

CONTINUED

22 CONTINUED: 22

The remark is not lost on Giles.

She goes to the wall to fetch the knives. He's in no hurry.

                    GILES
          Have you, uh, spoken with Dawn at all
          about the incident at Halloween?

                    BUFFY
          I thought you took care of that.

This one really registers. He stops, turns to look at her.
She doesn't get it.

                    GILES
          Right.

                    BUFFY
          What would I do without you.

She finishes stretching.

                    BUFFY (cont'd)
          Okay. I'm ready.

He turns to get the knives, singing:

                    GILES
          YOU'RE NOT READY FOR THE WORLD OUTSIDE
          YOU KEEP PRETENDING, BUT YOU JUST
          CAN'T HIDE
          I KNOW I SAID THAT I'D BE STANDING BY
          YOUR SIDE
          BUT I...

As he continues, he takes a couple of knives, weighs them in
his hand. He sings directly to Buffy and we realize now that
she isn't hearing a word he says. She twists her neck, sets
herself to deflect the knives. He hurls the first two as he
sings:

                    GILES (cont'd)
          YOUR PATH'S UNBEATEN, AND IT'S ALL
          UPHILL
          AND YOU CAN MEET IT, BUT YOU NEVER
          WILL
          AND I'M THE REASON THAT YOU'RE
          STANDING STILL
          BUT I....

And as he hits the chorus he hurls the last knife and it
stops, Matrix-like, right in front of her face.

                                              CONTINUED

22 CONTINUED: (2)   22

She bats it away, but everything is moving at extreme slow motion -- except for Giles.

                    GILES (cont'd)
          I WISH I COULD SAY THE RIGHT WORDS
          TO LEAD YOU THROUGH THIS LAND
          WISH I COULD PLAY THE FATHER
          AND TAKE YOU BY THE HAND
          WISH I COULD STAY
          BUT NOW I UNDERSTAND
          I'M STANDING IN THE WAY

We see her continuing to train throughout the rest of the number -- practicing flying kicks, working the bag, always in extreme slo mo, while Giles circles her at regular speed, watching.

                    GILES (cont'd)
          YOUR SISTER'S CRIES YOU WON'T HEAR AT
          ALL
          'CAUSE YOU KNOW I'M HERE TO TAKE THAT
          CALL
          SO YOU JUST LIE THERE, WHEN YOU
          SHOULD BE STANDING TALL
          BUT I...
          I WISH I COULD LAY YOUR ARMS DOWN
          AND LET YOU REST AT LAST
          WISH I COULD SLAY YOUR DEMONS
          BUT NOW THAT TIME HAS PASSED
          WISH I COULD STAY
          WE START WITH STANDING FAST
          BUT I'M STANDING IN THE WAY
          I'M JUST STANDING IN THE WAY

The number ends. Buffy turns to him.

                    BUFFY
          Did you say something?

He looks at her.

23 INT. THE MAGIC BOX - CONTINUING - NIGHT   23

Willow is heading into the cellar as Xander and Anya work behind the counter. There is unpleasant tension between the two of them.

Tara enters, in a rush.

                    ANYA
          Hey.

                                              CONTINUED

23 CONTINUED: 23

Tara barely nods, still moving, clearly wanting to avoid
Willow.

She moves quickly to the ladder, mounts it and starts looking
for a book. Pulling one out, she flips through the pages til
she finds:

CLOSE ON: AN ILLUSTRATION of the little weed she has, which
she now holds next to it. Below, the text: "Lethe's Bramble.
Used for augmenting spells of forgetting and mind control."

Willow emerges from the cellar with a book, stays at the
front of the store.

Tara looks at Willow, stricken. She sings, softly, and
unnoticed:

                    TARA
          I'M UNDER YOUR SPELL
          GOD, HOW CAN THIS BE
          PLAYING WITH MY MEMORY
          YOU KNOW I'VE BEEN THROUGH HELL
          WILLOW, DON'T YOU SEE
          THERE'LL BE NOTHING LEFT OF ME

Buffy enters the shop, crosses to Willow and begins (unheard)
talking to her. Giles follows her out entering frame below
Tara on his first line:

           TARA   GILES
     YOU MADE ME BELIEVE   BELIEVE ME I DON'T WANNA GO

               TARA/GILES
          AND IT'LL GRIEVE ME 'CAUSE I LOVE YOU
          SO
          BUT WE BOTH KNOW

An they start toward their respective loved ones, singing
soulfully, unheard by everyone, even each other.

           TARA   GILES
     WISH I COULD TRUST   WISH I COULD SAY
     THAT IT WAS JUST THIS ONCE THE RIGHT WORDS TO LEAD YOU
     BUT I MUST DO WHAT I MUST THROUGH THIS LAND
     I CAN'T ADJUST   WISH I COULD PLAY
     TO THIS DISGUST   THE FATHER AND TAKE YOU
     WE'RE DONE AND I JUST   BY THE HAND

               TARA/GILES
          WISH I COULD STAY
          WISH I COULD STAY
          WISH I COULD STAY
               (more)

                                            CONTINUED

23 CONTINUED: (2)   23

                    TARA/GILES (cont'd)
          WISH I COULD
          STAY

The final note rings out just as the front door flies open
and Spike shoves a henchman through.

                    SPIKE
          Lookie lookie what I found.

                    WILLOW
                (noticing finally)
          Tara?

                    TARA
          Is this the demon guy?

                    SPIKE
          Works for him. Has a nice little
          story for the Slayer, don't you?

He thrusts him forward again.

                    SPIKE (cont'd)
          Come on, then. Sing.

Music swells as the camera moves in on the henchman, who
takes a breath...

                    HENCHMAN
                (quickly and flatly)
          My master has the Slayer's sister
          hostage at the Bronze because she
          summoned him and at midnight he's
          gonna take her to the underworld to
          be his Queen.

                    GILES
          What does he want?

                    HENCHMAN
                (pointing to Buffy)
          Her. Plus chaos and insanity and
          people burning up, but that's more
          big picture stuff.

Spike grabs him from behind --

                    SPIKE
          If that's all you've got to say,
          then --

                                                    CONTINUED

23 CONTINUED: (3)   23

But he's flipped off by the henchman, who bolts out the still open door.

>   SPIKE (cont'd)
>   Strong. Someday he'll be a real
>   boy...

>   BUFFY
>   So Dawn's in trouble. It must be
>   Tuesday.

>   TARA
>   I just left her for a few minutes...

>   BUFFY
>   It's not your fault. Giles, what's
>   the plan?

>   XANDER
>   Plan, shman, let's mount up!

>   GILES
>   No.

They all turn to him, surprised.

>   ANYA
>   Uh, Dawn may have had the wrong idea
>   in summoning this creature but I've
>   seen some of these underworld child-
>   bride deals and they never end well.
>   Maybe once.

>   WILLOW
>   We're not just gonna stay here...

>   GILES
>   Yes we are. Buffy's going alone.

>   SPIKE
>   Don't be a stupid git, there's no --

>   GILES
>   When I want your opinion, Spike, I...
>   will never want your opinion.

>   WILLOW
>   A little confusion spell would --

>   TARA
>   No.

                                             CONTINUED

23 CONTINUED: (4)   23

Willow is surprised by the vehemence in her tone. So, in
fact, is Tara, who backs down a bit...

                    TARA (cont'd)
          I don't think that'll help.

                    SPIKE
          Forget them, Slayer, I got your back.

                    BUFFY
          I thought you wanted me to stay away
          from you. Isn't that what you sang?

She doesn't say it with much snideness, but Spike takes it
hard, looking embarrassedly about him.

                    XANDER
          Spikey sang a widdle song?

                    ANYA
                (earnestly)
          Would you say it was a breakaway pop
          hit, or more of a book number?

                    XANDER
          Let it go, sweetie.

                    SPIKE
          Fine. I hope you dance til you burn.
          You **and** the little bit.

He exits. Buffy turns to Giles.

                    BUFFY
          You're really not coming.

                    GILES
          It's up to you, Buffy.

                    BUFFY
          What do you expect me to do?

                    GILES
          Your best.

She looks around -- it's clear that everyone is going to back
Giles up. A beat, and she leaves.

24 EXT. STREET - NIGHT   24

(Note: for the purposes of this number, once a location is referred too, it will not be indicated again, 'cause it's intercutty city.)

Buffy walks to the Bronze, not particularly quickly. A few people dance by, very West Side Story/Absolute Beginners vibe -- fighting as much as dancing. There are some broken windows and a couple of trash fires. Low level chaos.

Buffy stands before a trashfire and puts her hand slowly out toward the flame.

                    BUFFY
                  (sings)
          I TOUCH THE FIRE AND IT FREEZES ME
          I LOOK INTO IT AND IT'S BLACK
          WHY CAN'T I FEEL
          MY SKIN SHOULD CRACK AND PEEL
          I WANT THE FIRE BACK

She starts off again...

                    BUFFY (cont'd)
          NOW THROUGH THE SMOKE SHE CALLS TO ME
          TO MAKE MY WAY ACROSS THE FLAME
          TO SAVE THE DAY
          OR MAYBE MELT AWAY
          I GUESS IT'S ALL THE SAME
          SO I WILL WALK THROUGH THE FIRE
          'CAUSE WHERE ELSE CAN I TURN
          I WILL WALK THROUGH THE FIRE
          AND LET IT --

25 EXT. ALLEY BEHIND THE MAGIC BOX - NIGHT   25

He is sitting with a cig, feeling mizzy.

                    SPIKE
                  (sings)
          THE TORCH I BEAR IS SCORCHING ME
          AND BUFFY'S LAUGHING I'VE NO DOUBT
          I HOPE SHE FRIES
          I'M FREE IF THAT BITCH DIES
                  (getting up)
          I'D BETTER HELP HER OUT

And off he goes.

26 INT. BRONZE - NIGHT   26

Sweet sings to Dawn, who sits in a corner.

                                              CONTINUED

26 CONTINUED: 26

                          SWEET
              SHE'S GETTING WARM -- IT BUILDS IN HER
              SHE MAY JUST GO UP IN A FLASH
              AND WHEN SHE'S DONE
              HER FRIENDS CAN HAVE THE FUN
              OF SIFTING THROUGH THE ASH

              SWEET   SPIKE
      CAUSE SHE IS DRAWN TO THE   'CAUSE SHE IS DRAWN TO THE
      FIRE   FIRE
      SOME PEOPLE NEVER LEARN   SHE WILL NEVER LEARN

                       SWEET/SPIKE
              AND SHE WILL WALK THROUGH THE FIRE
              AND LET IT

27 INT. THE MAGIC BOX - NIGHT   27

    The gang is there, each privately (or publicly) unhappy.

                          GILES
              WILL THIS DO A THING TO CHANGE HER
              AM I LEAVING DAWN IN DANGER
              IS MY SLAYER TOO FAR GONE TO CARE

                          XANDER
                       (to Giles)
              WHAT IF BUFFY CAN'T DEFEAT IT

                          ANYA
              BEADY-EYES IS RIGHT -- WE'RE NEEDED
              OR WE COULD JUST SIT AROUND AND GLARE

    They all get up to go, heading for the door --

                          GROUP
              WE'LL SEE IT THROUGH
              IT'S WHAT WE'RE ALWAYS HERE TO DO
              SO WE WILL WALK THROUGH THE FIRE

28 EXT. VARIOUS STREETS - NIGHT   28

    Buffy, Spike and the gang all get closer to the Bronze.

                          BUFFY
              SO ONE BY ONE THEY TURN FROM ME
              I GUESS MY FRIENDS CAN'T FACE THE COLD

                          TARA
              WHAT CAN'T WE FACE IF WE'RE TOGETHER

                                                    CONTINUED

28 CONTINUED: 28

                         BUFFY
              BUT WHY I FROZE
              NOT ONE AMONG THEM KNOWS
              AND NEVER CAN BE TOLD

                  ANYA   SWEET
         SHE CAME FROM THE GRAVE   SO ONE BY ONE THEY COME TO
         MUCH GRAVER   ME
                                      THE DISTANT REDNESS AS
                  SPIKE   THEIR GUIDE
         FIRST I'LL KILL HER THEN   BUT WHAT THEY'LL FIND
         I'LL SAVE HER   AIN'T WHAT THEY HAVE IN MIND
                                      IT'S WHAT THEY HAVE INSIDE

                  TARA
         EVERYTHING IS TURNING OUT   BUFFY
         SO DARK   GOING THROUGH THE MOTIONS
                                      WALKING THROUGH THE PART
                  SPIKE
         NO I'LL SAVE HER THEN I'LL   SWEET
         KILL HER   SHE WILL COME TO ME

                  WILLOW
         I THINK THIS LINE'S MOSTLY
         FILLER

                  GILES
         WHAT'S IT GONNA TAKE TO
         STRIKE A SPARK

                  BUFFY
         THESE ENDLESS DAYS
         ARE FINALLY ENDING IN A
         BLAZE

29 EXT. OUTSIDE THE BRONZE - NIGHT   29

     Is where Buffy ends up (alone) as they all sing:

                    BUFFY, SPIKE AND GROUP
              AND WE ARE CAUGHT IN THE FIRE
              THE POINT OF NO RETURN
              SO WE WILL WALK THROUGH THE FIRE
              AND LET IT BURN
              LET IT BURN
              LET IT BURN
              LET IT BURN

30 INT. BRONZE - NIGHT   30

     On the last note, Buffy KICKS the door of the Bronze off its
     hinges (or at least open -- that's a big door).

                                                       CONTINUED

30 CONTINUED: 30

EXTREME CLOSE UP: SWEET'S SMILE

                    SWEET
          Showtime...

                                              BLACK OUT.

                    END OF ACT THREE

ACT FOUR

31 INT. BRONZE - NIGHT   31

Buffy walks slowly in to find Sweet seated on stage, Dawn on
the floor leaning up against his chair, almost like an exotic
slavegirl.

The henchmen are in the shadows, surrounding Buffy, getting
closer...

                    SWEET
          I love a good entrance.

                    BUFFY
          How are you with death scenes?

He laughs.

                    BUFFY (cont'd)
          You got a name?

                    SWEET
          I got a hundred.

                    BUFFY
          Well, I aughta know what to call you
          if you're gonna be my brother in law.

                    DAWN
          Buffy I swear I didn't do it.

                    BUFFY
          Don't worry, you're not going
          anywhere. I am.

                    DAWN
          What?

                    BUFFY
              (to Sweet)
          What do you want a little kid for?
          Deal's this: I can't kill you, you
          take me to hellsville in her place.

                    SWEET
          What if I kill you?

                    BUFFY
          Trust me. It won't help.

                    SWEET
          That's gloomy.

                                              CONTINUED

31 CONTINUED: 31

                              BUFFY
                    That's life.

He rises, starts down the steps as his henchmen get closer to
Buffy.

                              SWEET
                    Come now, is that really what you
                    feel? Isn't life a miraculous thing?

                              BUFFY
                    I think you already know...
                         (sings)
                    LIFE'S A SHOW AND WE ALL PLAY OUR
                    PARTS
                    AND WHEN THE MUSIC STARTS
                    WE OPEN UP OUR HEARTS
                    IT'S ALL RIGHT IF SOMETHING'S COME
                    OUT WRONG
                    WE'LL SING A HAPPY SONG

She looks at the camera with an ironic, battleworn smile...

                              BUFFY (cont'd)
                    AND YOU CAN SING ALONG

She sings -- and attacks the henchmen at the same time,
punctuating each happy platitude with a gruelling blow.

                              BUFFY (cont'd)
                    WHERE THERE'S LIFE THERE'S HOPE
                    EVERY DAY'S A GIFT
                    WISHES CAN COME TRUE
                    WHISTLE WHILE YOU WORK
                    SO HARD
                    ALL DAY
                    TO BE LIKE OTHER GIRLS
                    TO FIT INTO THIS GLITTERING WORLD

She's finished them off, turns to Sweet --

ANGLE: THE GANG

Enter, see the sitch. Giles takes command.

                              GILES
                    She needs backup. Tara. Anya.

They go, while the other three circle around. But all Tara
and Anya do is get behind Buffy and sing back up AAAAHHHs.

                                              CONTINUED

31 CONTINUED: (2)   31

                    BUFFY
          DON'T GIVE ME SONGS
          DON'T GIVE ME SONGS
          GIVE ME SOMETHING TO SING ABOUT
          I NEED SOMETHING TO SING ABOUT

She notices the gang, splits her attention as she sings to
everyone and no one:

                    BUFFY (cont'd)
          LIFE'S A SHOW YOU DON'T GET TO
          REHEARSE
          AND EVERY SINGLE VERSE
          CAN MAKE IT THAT MUCH WORSE
          STILL MY FRIENDS DON'T KNOW WHY I
          IGNORE
          THE MILLION THINGS OR MORE
          I SHOULD BE DANCING FOR
          ALL THE JOYS LIFE SENDS
          FAMILY AND FRIENDS
          ALL THE TWISTS AND BENDS
          KNOWING THAT IT ENDS
          WELL THAT
          DEPENDS
          ON IF THEY LET YOU GO
          ON IF THEY KNOW ENOUGH TO KNOW
          THAT WHEN YOU'VE BOWED
          YOU LEAVE THE CROWD

She's about to go into the chorus -- but the energy goes from
her. She can hardly look at her friends. Tara and Anya have
backed off.

Spike enters, takes it all in, stonefaced.

                    BUFFY (cont'd)
          THERE WAS NO PAIN
          NO FEAR, NO DOUBT
          TIL THEY PULLED ME OUT OF HEAVEN
          SO THAT'S MY REFRAIN
          I LIVE IN HELL
          'CAUSE I WAS EXPELLED FROM HEAVEN
          I THINK I WAS IN HEAVEN

She turns to Sweet, vehement --

                    BUFFY (cont'd)
          SO GIVE ME SOMETHING TO SING ABOUT
          PLEASE GIVE ME SOMETHING...

She starts dancing, giving herself up to it, faster and
faster -- until she begins, literally, to smoke.

                                              CONTINUED

31 CONTINUED: (3)   31

She's spinning -- about to combust -- when she is physically
stopped by Spike. He holds her arms for a moment as the
smoke wafts around them, the danger past.

                         SPIKE
               LIFE'S NOT A SONG
               LIFE ISN'T BLISS
               LIFE IS JUST THIS: IT'S LIVING
               YOU'LL GET ALONG
               THE PAIN THAT YOU FEEL
               YOU ONLY CAN HEAL BY LIVING
               YOU HAVE TO GO ON LIVING
               SO ONE OF US IS LIVING

                         DAWN
               The hardest thing in this world is to
               live in it.

There is affection, but also toughness in the way she parrots
Buffy's phrase back at her.

ANGLE: WILLOW is quietly crying, overwhelmed by the
implications of what she's done. Tara hovers, wanting to
comfort her, but still in her own pain as well.

                         SWEET
               Now that was a showstopper. Not
               quite the fireworks I was looking
               for --

                         WILLOW
               Get out of here.

There is such quiet vehemence in her voice -- and the look on
her face is shared by pretty much everybody.

                         SWEET
               Hmm, I smell power. I guess the
               little missus and I should be on our
               way.

                         GILES
               That's never gonna happen.

                         SWEET
               I don't make the rules; she summoned
               me.

                         DAWN
               I so did not! He keeps saying that!

                                                        CONTINUED

31 CONTINUED: (4)   31

                    SWEET
          You've got my talisman on, sweet
          thing.

Dawn looks down at the necklace, realizes.

                    DAWN
          Oh! But -- no! I just -- this at
          the Magic Box... on the floor, and I
          was cleaning and I forgot to... But
          I didn't summon anything.

                    SWEET
          Well now, that's a twist.

                    GILES
          If it was at the shop, that means one
          of us had to...

ANGLE: THE GROUP

For a beat, we wait to see who did it.

In the background, Xander raises his hand.

                    ANYA
          Xander?

                    XANDER
          I didn't know what was gonna happen!
          I just heard, you know, revelries and
          song and... I wanted to be sure we'd
          work out. Get a happy ending.

Sweet laughs. Big time.

                    SWEET
          And I think it worked out just fine.

                    XANDER
          Does this mean I have to... be your
          queen?

                    SWEET
          It's tempting. But I think we'll
          waive that clause just this once.
          Big smiles, everyone: you beat the
          bad guy!
                    (sings)
          WHAT A LOT OF FUN
          YOU GUYS HAVE BEEN SWELL
          AND THERE'S NOT A ONE

                                              CONTINUED

31 CONTINUED: (5)   31

                         SWEET (cont'd)
                WHO CAN SAY THIS ENDED WELL
                ALL THOSE SECRETS YOU BEEN CONCEALING
                SAY YOU'RE HAPPY NOW -- ONCE MORE
                WITH FEELING
                WELL I GOTTA RUN
                SEE YOU ALL IN HELL

He disappears right at the last line, the final two words
ringing out from emptiness.

There is silence.

The group all stand about, each of them more alone than
they've ever been. Finally, tentatively, Dawn begins:

                         DAWN
                WHERE DO WE GO FROM HERE

And others join in...

                         BUFFY/SPIKE
                WHERE DO WE GO FROM HERE

                         GILES
                THE BATTLE'S DONE AND WE KIND OF WON

                         TARA/GILES
                SO WE SOUND OUR VICT'RY CHEER
                WHERE DO WE GO FROM HERE

                         XANDER/ANYA
                WHY IS THE PATH UNCLEAR
                WHEN WE KNOW HOME IS NEAR

                         GROUP (cont'd)
                UNDERSTAND WE'LL GO HAND IN HAND
                BUT WE'LL WALK ALONE IN FEAR
                TELL ME, WHERE DO WE GO FROM HERE

At this point the beat picks up and the gang starts moving in
sync, the big finish beginning... Spike moving with the
group --

                         GROUP (cont'd)
                WHEN DOES "THE END" APPEAR
                WHEN DO THE TRUMPETS CHEER
                THE CURTAINS CLOSE ON A KISS -- GOD
                KNOWS
                WE CAN --

                                                  CONTINUED

31 CONTINUED: (6)   31

Suddenly, Spike realizes what he's doing.

                    SPIKE
          Bugger this.

And heads out as the rest continue...

                    GROUP
          -- TELL THE END IS NEAR
          WHERE DO WE GO FROM HERE

32 EXT. OUTSIDE THE BRONZE - CONTINUING - NIGHT   32

We can here music continue faintly from inside as Spike heads
down the alley, stopped by:

                    BUFFY
          Hey.

He turns, uncertain of what she wants.

                    SPIKE
          You should go back in. Finish the
          big group sing, get your KoombaYa-
          Ya's out.

                    BUFFY
          I don't want to...

                    SPIKE
          Day you suss out what you do want,
          there'll probably be a parade.
          Seventy six bloody trombones.

                    BUFFY
          Spike, I...

                    SPIKE
          Look, you don't have to say anything.
          We both know I can talk enough for
          both of --

          BUFFY   ?
I TOUCH THE FIRE AND IT
FREEZES ME
I LOOK INTO IT AND IT'S   SPIKE
BLACK   I DIED SO MANY YEARS AGO
THIS ISN'T REAL   BUT YOU CAN MAKE ME FEEL...
BUT I JUST WANT TO FEEL...

                                                    CONTINUED

32 CONTINUED: 32

They are moving closer as they sing, interrupting whatever thoughts they were going to finish with a sudden, passionate, kiss. The music (and who can blame it) swells, and we hear a final:

                    GROUP (O.S.)
          WHERE DO WE GO FROM HERE...

And over the continuing kiss appear the words THE END (with the old style "A Twentieth Century Fox Television Release" beneath it). Curtains close as the music crescendos, ringing out as we

BLACKOUT.

                    END OF SHOW

"Life's a Show"

Musical Terminology from the Script

Buffy and her friends find their sudden musical stylings to be fun yet disturbing, and easily settle into the banter of students of musical theater. Here's a little primer for the viewers who may not be as familiar with the terminology taken from the stage directions and dialogue.

There will be an overture that runs the length of the opening credits: An instrumental composition intended as an introduction to the larger work, usually comprised of brief pieces of the songs from the musical

Once more, with feeling: Traditional phrase heard during rehearsals indicating that the singer should perform the song again, with more emotion behind the singing

Every single night, the same arrangement: This line has dual meaning, as it is more than just Buffy's regret for the rut her life seems to be in. It also refers to a musical composition being adapted for other instruments or voices.

Walking through the part: Refers to an actor going over her lines and actions without emotionally connecting to the role

. . . and there were **harmonies:** A combination of musical notes or sounds in such a way as to produce a pleasing effect

*. . . and a dance with coconut*s: Possible reference to Carmen Miranda style tropical dance numbers popularized in the Twentieth Century Fox musicals of the 1940s

. . . and we're all stuck inside his wacky **Broadway** *nightmare:* The New York street (and section of the city surrounding the street) in which most musicals and theatrical straight plays make their formal American debut. While Willow sings this line, Tara places her hands out on either side of her body, spreading her fingers and shaking them repeatedly. This move is commonly referred to as "jazz hands" and is an overused device in musical choreography that has become a bit of a joke in recent years.

. . . **the orchestration backing her . . . :** The music playing beneath the lyrics

It's the end of a huge production number: A dance number usually consisting of a large group of characters

That's Entertainment: Song from the musical *The Bandwagon*

That last note is entirely discordant: A harsh, sour sound

This is my **verse,** *hello:* A section or stanza of a musical composition

They collapse onto the sofa, laughing in classic post-musical number style: See "Good Mornin'" from the movie musical *Singin' in the Rain* as one such popular example.

I felt like we were being watched, like a wall was missing from our apartment, like there were only three walls, no **fourth wall:** Anya is referring to the practice in which most plays and television shows are blocked wherein the audience is watching the action through a non-existent "fourth wall." When an actor is said to "break the fourth wall," she is speaking directly to the audience, much in the way Anya and Xander performed the number "I'll Never Tell."

Plus our number was clearly a **retro pastiche** *that's never going to be a* **breakaway pop hit:** Phrase used by Anya to describe the above-mentioned title. Oftentimes in musicals, a signature song breaks out beyond the confines of the musical and becomes popular among the mass audience. Unfortunately Xander and Anya's piece, which imitates an old-school musical style, would probably have a difficult time transitioning onto the Top 40.

. . . while the police were taking witness **arias:** Solo vocal pieces with instrumental accompaniment

Six-hundred-pound Chorago demon making like **Yma Sumac:** Spike is referring to a noted Peruvian singer, known for her incredible vocal range.

. . . some **Lord of the Dance**—*but not the scary one*: Michael Flatley, famous Irish dancer whose stage show is also titled *Lord of the Dance*, became an international sensation in the nineties.

I'm the heart of **swing:** Pertaining to a musical style of the 1930s based on big-band jazz

I'm the "Twist and Shout": Famous song performed by The Beatles, originally released in 1963

. . . these **melodies:** The leading part of a musical composition

And still have time to get a **soft-shoe** *in*: A form of tap dancing performed without metal taps worn on the shoes

. . . this whole session is going to turn into a **training montage from an eighties movie:** See *Rocky III* and "The Eye of the Tiger"

Well if we hear any **inspirational power chords** . . . : Reference to the strum of the strings from an electric guitar in those inspirational rock songs from the eighties

As he hits the chorus . . . : Section of a song providing the main theme, which is repeated at intervals

Would you say it was more of a **breakaway pop hit** *or more of a* **book number:** A book number is a musical piece written largely to progress the plot, as opposed to a stand-alone number that can be understood separate from the larger work and released to the general public.

A few people dance by, very *West Side Story* **(1)/***Absolute Beginners* **(2):** (1) Updated musical version of *Romeo and Juliet* set in New York in the fifties. The musical-turned-movie is particularly known for its dance sequences originally choreographed by Jerome Robbins (2) A musical film adaptation of Colin MacInnes's novel about a boy in late 1950s London who falls in love with a model

I think this line's mostly **filler:** Reference to a line of dialogue or song that serves no overall purpose in progressing the plot

She needs **backup:** Background singers

So that's my **refrain:** A phrase of verse repeated throughout a song

Now, that was a **show stopping number:** A production number in a musical that is so well received by the crowd that the show momentarily stops while the audience applauds wildly (commonly referred to as simply "a showstopper")

At this point the beat picks up: The rhythm of a musical piece

Get your koomba ya-ya's out: Koombaya (also spelled Kumbaya) is a traditional folksong, often sung around a campfire.

Seventy-six bloody trombones: Reference to a breakaway pop hit (or, more accurately, breakaway marching band hit) from the musical *The Music Man*

The music (and who can blame it) swells: Common ending to a musical in which the orchestral music rises and intensifies, usually to underscore a kiss

And over the continuing kiss appear the words THE END (with the old-style "A Twentieth Century Fox Television Release" beneath it): Traditional final visual from the famous Twentieth Century Fox Motion Pictures releases such as *Hello Dolly*, *State Fair*, *Carousel*, and *The Sound of Music*

Behind
the Scenes

"I've Got a Theory"

Music has been an integral part of theater since the foundation of the dramatic art form in Ancient Greece. Through thousands of years of theatrical development, opera and musical theater evolved along with the dramatic and comic counterparts. This ultimately led to the so-called "Broadway-style" musicals popularized in the twentieth century. When cinema came along and developed the "talking pictures," one of the first of the "talkies" was a musical entitled *The Jazz Singer*. Likewise, the early days of television included a fair amount of musical television in the musical variety show format.

Musicals found a sporadic place throughout the history of television. On a few occasions, entire series have developed around the musical format of such shows as *Fame* in the eighties and the short-lived series *Cop Rock* in 1990. Alternately, several television series have done special episodes where the characters suddenly burst into song. However, these have predominately been found in comedy series and have often been met with mixed reviews. When a series breaks from its regular format, there is always a difficult challenge to be met, whether it is dealing with the addition of music or some other groundbreaking technique.

Buffy the Vampire Slayer episodes like "Hush," "The Body," and "Once More, With Feeling" all qualify as challenging standout episodes and, not so coincidentally, are each written and directed by *Buffy* series creator, **Joss Whedon**. As he explains, "The episodes where I break the traditional format of the show are never an attempt at a stunt, because I don't like things that are just stunts. I think stunts take you out of the narrative and they become more important than the show. I would never do something like a black-and-white episode that's just about the film and not about our guys and what they're going through."

While these episodes do break the established format of the series in such a way as to underscore the story line, there is also a more technical reason, as Joss goes on to explain. "I never approach these episodes wondering what can I do that will be intense and will blow everybody away. It's more like me trying to find out what I'm doing wrong. I came to 'Hush' because I felt that I was becoming lazy as a director. I thought that I needed to push myself visually. That evolved into the question, 'What if I had no choice?'"

The convenient part about being a writer and director is that when one aspect needs to be challenged, the other can come in and provide the motivation for change. Joss recalls that the intensity of "The Body" grew out of a comment from **Sarah Michelle Gellar** regarding the fact that he was just going to cut away to music instead of playing a scene out emotionally in a previous episode. At the time, Joss could not disagree. "I started to think that sometimes, when I don't get what I want out of a performance, I do just add music. But that's another way of getting lazy as a director. So I decided to take that crutch away, because the story I was breaking lent itself to a formal exercise that evolved into me thinking 'What if I only had one scene per act and I didn't give people an out?' I don't cut away. I don't cut to the music. I don't do anything that lets them get away from the fact of this death."

The idea behind "Once More, With Feeling," however, did not grow solely out of a challenging means of storytelling. This episode was the closest to a personal indulgence that Joss has had with the series. "I've always loved musicals," he admits with pride. "I grew up with musicals in stage and movies." And he did literally grow up with musicals, playing parts in a variety of shows in his youth, including high school productions of *West Side Story* and *How to Succeed in Business Without Really Trying.*

"I'm a Sondheim fanatic, born and bred. I know every show of his backward." He refers to the famous lyricist Stephen Sondheim whose award winning works include *West Side Story*, *Gypsy*, *Sweeney Todd*, and *Into the Woods*, among many others. The list of Joss's influences goes on to include Frank Loesser (*Guys and Dolls*, *Most Happy Fella*, *How to Succeed in Business . . .*), Jerry Bock and Sheldon Harnick (*Fiorello!*, *Fiddler on the Roof*), Stephen Schwartz (*Godspell*, *Pippin*), and the musicals *Rent* and *It's a Bird, It's a Plane, It's Superman.* "The poppier musicals were also big influences," he adds. "As a child of the seventies, you can't get past those." His tastes also go back to include the old school movie musicals of the mid-twentieth century.

It was another writer—one who is not traditionally associated with musicals—who provided the largest influence on getting a musical episode of *Buffy the Vampire Slayer* on the air: William Shakespeare. Joss

missed the acting he had not done since high school, so he started hosting informal Sunday night Shakespeare readings at his home with some of the writers and cast members of *Buffy* and *Angel*. Knowing that one of his guests, **Anthony Stewart Head**, was also an accomplished singer, Joss managed to convince him to sing at one of the readings. This led to other guests singing around the piano, including **Amber Benson** and her sister performing a song that the actress had written. Later, **James Marsters** brought a guitar to one of the gatherings and not only impressed Joss, but helped an idea begin to take form.

For Joss, these impromptu talent nights were rich with possibilities. But it took a combination of the right factors to fall into place that led to the development of the musical episode. "All of a sudden I'm presented with all of this singing talent," Joss says. "This had all started in the fall of season five, and that [next] summer I was going to take a few months off, which I had not done since before the series began. I had always said I wouldn't do a musical because it would take six months." As fate would have it, Joss was about to have the six months that he needed.

"At the end of season five," he continues, "we were in a position we've never been in before. We had really gotten ahead. Usually at the beginning of a season we're scrambling desperately to get stories broken and we're way behind. But here, we were actually able to break the first few stories of the following season before I left for vacation. The musical was number six."

When attempting such an undertaking, Joss notes the importance of working one step at a time. "You have to break the stories chronologically. We knew what the general arc for the season was going to be." Joss also knew that the arc of the characters growing up and making their way in the world wasn't going to launch in the first few episodes. That would be the time to establish the characters and set up themes. It would be the sixth episode where all those themes would tie together and start the emotional arc on its way.

As he headed for vacation, Joss had a detailed outline of the first six episodes. "When I started writing the musical I knew exactly where everybody was emotionally and what had to break," he explains. "I knew that this would be the episode where Buffy told her friends that she'd been in Heaven and all the other truths would come out."

Joss continues to refer to his "vacation," and while he did spend time with his wife, Kai Cole, relaxing in Cape Cod, much of his downtime was focused on the challenges of writing the musical. "I knew it was hard enough to write a new script, but to make one rhyme and put music to it when I could barely play the piano or the guitar—that would be hard. But here I had this vacation, so I actually started learning to play guitar because I thought some of this would need to be written on the guitar and some on the piano. Then I spent my entire vacation banging out these tunes."

Though it was not his first time creating songs, Joss admits that it was tough going to be doing something on such a grand scale. "I'd written songs before, to play for my friends, but to write a musical is really tough because you have to explain a [lot] of stuff while writing and trying to be clever. You have to write a show where the songs *were* the plot and everything that was important in the show had to happen during the songs."

Joss was adamant that the writing be focused on marrying the songs to the plot. "I get very cranky about TV shows that do musical episodes that are basically variety shows where they play a scene and then they'll sing an oldie that has something vaguely to do with the scene, but the scene is over already. There's no reason to sing. And that's the thing about musicals that most people have forgotten on TV. It's not the only thing that was wrong with a show like *Cop Rock*, but it was one of the things. They would play a scene out and then sing about it instead of just playing the scene with song."

Ready to accept the challenge, Joss sat down at his piano and with his guitar. He already had an idea of the cast's abilities from their Sunday night gatherings, which helped in divvying up the musical numbers, creating the music for the pieces and tying them to the story outline. "I built the entire plot around people's strengths and styles, and their needs and desires. For example, **Michelle Trachtenberg** wanted to dance but was not that comfortable singing, so I put in the ballet for her that **Chris Beck** actually wrote the music to. I knew Tony was going to be my ballad guy and that Amber was going to be my breakaway pop hit girl, because I had to have the breakaway pop hit."

He knew the abilities of those performers, along with **Emma Caulfield** and James Marsters, and how they would fit into what he had planned. However, the rest of the cast—Sarah Michelle Gellar, **Alyson Hannigan**, and **Nicholas Brendon**—were equally important factors whose talents he was not as familiar with. Joss goes on to explain, "Sarah was a bit of an unknown because she had never sung before. Aly was like, '*Don't make me sing!*' while Nick's attitude was, 'Well, I've never sung a note, but I'll do whatever you like.' I tried to find something for everything."

After four months of pounding away at the keys and strumming the guitar, Joss had the backbone of the musical, but the work had just begun. "When I was done I had about seven pages left of actual script to write because I'd written the entire show in song form. The whole process took about six months. It took about four months of writing and then when I came back it was two months of recording, sound mixing, producing, arranging, and dance rehearsals."

"What can't we face?"

When Joss Whedon returned from vacation, he not only had the script with him, but he also had another aid in bringing his vision to reality. "I actually recorded the entire soundtrack with my wife in Cape Cod," he explains. "That's when everybody found out what I already knew, which is that she has an extraordinary voice. People would listen to the recording and say to me, 'God, your wife can really sing . . . and . . . and your wife can really sing.' [He laughs.] Then they would say about my singing, 'I forgive you' and 'keep your day job.'"

Just because the music had been put to the songs did not mean that the musical was ready to be filmed. Joss knew that his basic score would need to be formally arranged for orchestra and band, but while his tal-

ents seemed to be ever growing, he knew that he would need help. After turning to composers **Jesse Tobias** and Christophe Beck to produce and arrange the songs, they began working at building on what was already there.

Chris recalls the first meeting of the musical trio as they went over the script with Joss and Kai's rough track. "We talked about the musical direction of each song from a stylistic and arranging perspective. Joss had really specific ideas. He knew, for example, that he wanted 'Going Through the Motions' to be a big Disney thing. He knew that for Spike's song he wanted a big modern rock sound. For a guy who doesn't have any formal training, I was honestly shocked at the amount of clear thought and vision that he had for each song."

From there, the musicians set to work formulating their plan of attack. Jesse explains, "Joss had the idea for bringing Chris and I together because we would cover where one of us might not be as experienced as the other. It broke down easily for us. From the rough ideas that Joss had given us and our own follow up conversations, we knew who would be responsible for bringing in what aspects and how we would divvy up the work from there."

Chris adds that the process was quite collaborative all the way through. "The basic idea was that Jesse handled the rockier numbers and I handled the numbers that involved things like big band or orchestra. A third of the songs were rock band songs without too much else; another third was a combination of rock elements and other elements; and a last third didn't have much in the way of rock elements at all." But just because they had split the work did not mean they had split the focus. Chris continues, "Even though we divvied them up that way at first, we were both heavily involved in everything."

Jesse also remembers that Joss was never far from the arranging process and echoes Chris's opinion of the novice musician. "Joss went to all the recordings and was at a lot of the overdub sessions. He had some really great input as far as sounds. And it was pretty advanced stuff, like the chord changes and his vision on the end piece. It was pretty amazing for somebody who is not a musician himself."

Naturally the process had begun in a very logical way, with rough-sounding backing tracks in the computer. Chris explains, "When I say rough, I mean really rough. There were no live instruments of any kind. It was just with a drum machine and samplers playing guitar parts, just to get an idea of tempo and key to make sure that the general feel of the song was right. Once that was done, we spent many, many, many hours at my studio with Jesse laying down guitar tracks and bass tracks and anything else that we could come up with. I think there was a part that Jesse played on an old cheesy Casio sampler that ultimately didn't make the final cut of the show. It was really sort of "anything goes." When the songs started to take a little more shape, we got ready to plan our sessions. We really had two big sessions for recording the music."

The first of the sessions was held at **Grandmaster Studio** in Hollywood. As Jesse explains, Grandmaster "is a great studio from the seventies," where many famous artists recorded, including **Stevie Wonder**. This first session covered the rockier tunes that were under Jesse's jurisdiction. He played the guitar and called on **Josh Freese**, from the band A Perfect Circle and bass player **Steven McDonald** from Redd Cross, to record the tracks live together.

With the band in place, Jesse and the guys started working. "We loaded in at ten o'clock," Jesse continues. "Everything went late, like it always does, so we didn't really start digging into the tunes until about one. I think we had thirteen to fifteen songs that we wanted to lay some rhythm tracks down on. We just set up the sheet music and started recording as many of the songs as we could straight through."

Both Joss and Chris sat in on much of the session, and Jesse was glad to have their input. "It was great because Joss was walking around in the recording booth giving us direction and different suggestions for the feel of the song," he notes. "It turned out really great. I couldn't believe the amount of stuff that we actually covered. We just went through and laid down rhythm tracks for everything."

A second session with a big band was called for under Chris's leadership. "That work is most prominently featured in Anya and Xander's song 'I'll Never Tell,'" he recalls. "It was also in some of the demon's numbers and the jazzier stuff. Once we had all of that, the big task was recording all the vocals."

With two different musicians overseeing two different recording sessions, it could have been difficult to form musical cohesion. But Jesse and Chris worked closely together to ensure that the sound was the same. "Chris and I played a lot of the guitar, piano, and strings through the musical," Jesse explains. "And that lent to the continuity since we were playing a lot of those key instruments through the whole thing. A lot of the rock numbers still have strings and keyboards too. That's what I think really held it together. When I listen back to it, the entire show really has that feel to me that it's one group of musicians playing through the whole thing."

Chris agrees. "I think that kind of cohesiveness is going to happen anytime there's really one person or one team of likeminded people who are working on one thing all the way through. I think the songs are really different styles, and I think, even more than any work that Jesse and I did, what holds it all together is the story and the lyrics and the way it all flows."

In addition to producing and arranging the music, Chris was also responsible for creating the score for the episode. The score consisted of the instrumental pieces between songs as well as Dawn's dance number. But Chris admits that even the score for the episode came from the original vision. "Joss wanted it to be like a traditional musical, so whenever possible all the incidental music is based on melodies from Joss's songs, like the overture at the beginning. For instance, there's an intro when Tara and Dawn are having the conversation up in

Dawn's bedroom. When Tara realizes that Willow put a whammy on her to make her forget, you hear a little remnant of 'Under Your Spell' before we go into Dawn's song."

Since Chris hadn't actually worked on the series in a year and a half prior to the episode, he refrained from using any of the themes he had previously established for the characters. The thinking for this was also due to the stand-alone aspect of the episode. And, although the tunes did not noticeably pop up in the score for subsequent episodes, Chris was pleased to note that he heard Buffy whistling one of her songs a few episodes later.

Coexecutive Producer **Marti Noxon** remembers the intense schedule of preparing for the show. "It was the most involved episode we've ever done in terms of time. We had more man hours involved from the actors' point of view than we've had in any episode ever. Each one of them had to do a pretty extensive amount of work before they ever stood before the camera. By the time things were actually being filmed, they were so well prodded and rehearsed that the actual shooting of it went rather smoothly."

While the music tracks were being lain, the episode continued to take shape in other areas as well. Considering the unique nature of the episode, a substantial amount of work needed to be done, including laying down the vocal tracks and rehearsing the dance numbers. Most *Buffy* episodes are shot on an eight day schedule, but the producers knew that "Once More, With Feeling" was going to take considerably more time.

To accommodate the needs of the episode, a rehearsal schedule was set so that the actors could be working on their singing, dancing, and recording while in the process of shooting the episodes leading up to "Once More, With Feeling." The first five episodes of the season were scheduled so that whenever an actor had free time, she or he could be working on some element of the musical. To accommodate the schedule, episode five ("All the Way") featured Dawn heavily so the other actors could focus on the final preparations for the musical. Then, once Michelle's work was done on that episode, she was given extra time to prepare for her dance.

While all the rehearsing and preparations were underway, there was another unique element involved in the rehearsals for this episode: Everything was being recorded for posterity. Coexecutive Producer **David Fury** had taken it upon himself to videotape the entire development process. It was his behind-the-scenes video that UPN used in the commercials advertising the upcoming episode.

"I videotaped the making of everything," David explains. "Once I heard the score and read Joss's script, I realized this was going to be really important. It wasn't just a novelty episode of the series. I thought it was something really great and special. I didn't know what was going to be done to promote it, but I thought that someone needed to document the making of it because I felt it was pretty monumental. So I asked Joss if it would be all right to sit it on all the production meetings and go to all the rehearsals, recordings, and everything just to tape it."

Of course Joss agreed, and David set to work documenting everything from laying down the music tracks to dance rehearsals and even the breaks in between. "There was about thirty-five to forty hours of video," he says. After the episode aired, David set to work on editing it together and produced a companion documentary for the musical.

As he was there for the entire rehearsal process, David is the prime person to detail the events. "The first thing that was done was that Joss needed to get everyone's voice recorded. Most of the actors were given tapes of the demo that Joss had made with his wife, Kai, which is a collector's item right there because Kai is an incredible singer. Just hearing the two of them with Joss playing piano with occasional guitar was really special. That's what the actors took with them to learn their songs. Then they came into the studio and each of them worked on their numbers one after the other. After that there was the choreography rehearsal for those doing dance moves."

Chris Beck remembers how seriously everyone took the process of preparing for the episode. "Basically, the entire cast kind of panicked when they found out Joss was going to do this. Some of them took it upon themselves to find coaching. **Sally Stevens**, who is a vocal coach and vocal contractor, helped several members of the cast while they were doing their recording sessions. Anytime that we had an actor in the recording studio, she was here, except in the cases of the actors who had a lot of experience, like Tony. He doesn't need any help from anybody. He sounds perfectly great without any effort. Different members of the cast relied on the coaching differently."

Sally's work was not solely restricted to coaching. Being a vocal contractor as well, she was the one who put the production together with the handful of professional singers that were brought in to do some of the bit parts, like the villains in the song "Going Through the Motions."

Chris continues to look back on the process with fondness. "As a score composer, we hardly work with the actors directly at all. After we did a little bit of searching around we realized that the best place to do the vocals was my studio because it was always available. It was only a few blocks from the sound stages where they shoot the show, so it was also very convenient. Whenever an actor had a little bit of time, they would come by and we would do as much work as we could with them."

However, Chris remembers that producing a musical with several untrained singers did have its fair amount of early stresses. Luckily he found that the concerns were easily allayed. "There was this fun and tense moment when we first brought in a member of the cast. They would put on their headphones and stand in front of the microphone while we'd get the song ready. It was always this incredibly tense moment when we wondered how it was going to sound. In every case, with every actor, once we heard the first notes we just looked at each other and smiled because we knew everything was going to be fine."

The chances they were taking in developing a musical around several actors who were not professionally trained singers paid off in a big way. Chris continues, "Before that moment there were a few cast members that none of us had heard sing at all. Even the ones that had minimal training and minimal experience like Alyson, who has very few lines in the episode, equipped herself really well on her two or three lines. One of her lines is even a self-referential joke about how little she's singing. And the whole thing just comes off great. The way that all the cast was able to give it their all, even if they didn't have a trained voice, was great. For example, Nick's singing and dancing--clearly he had no training, but he enthused his performance with so much excitement and energy it just made up for it."

Once the songs were recorded, the work on the dancing began. As with every other element of the musical, Joss admits, "I was very specific about what I wanted. And I was lucky because the choreographer, **Adam Shankman**, and assistant choreographer, **Anne "Mama" Fletcher**, were just really great. They were very imaginative but also flexible, and they brought a huge amount to the party. Dance is actually my favorite thing, and there isn't really that much dance in the show. Amateurs can sing, but dancing is a lot tougher."

Adam Shankman agrees that the dancing was a challenge, but not because of the actors' abilities. "Everybody was so game to do the work, but the problem was that there was very little time in the schedule. Everything had to be tailored to each cast member and what they were able to do in the time frame that we were given to do it. That meant I couldn't go out there and do anything too complicated. But with the assistance of the trained extras and the work of the cast, it looks like more than it was."

Adam found that the benefit of coming in when he did was that a lot of the prep work had been done. "The actors were already familiar with the music because they had already recorded it and sung through it. I had taken a week to sketch what each number was going to be with my assistant and Joss. Then the actors came in when they had a few hours and we would just put them right into it. There was no training or anything. It was simply a matter of maximizing on what the actors did best. If I saw that the cast was weaker in one area or stronger in another, I would just tailor my work to whatever they could do, because I needed to make them as comfortable as possible.

"My philosophy of choreography is very simple in that every piece of music is a road map," Adam goes on to say. "When you're doing musical theater, you're assisting the narrative, not trying to work against it. Anything that helped sell the story was how I approached it and then the music tells you how the characters should move. Plus Joss was extremely specific about what he wanted to see. Each piece of material was written in such a specific style that it guided the choreography."

Whether it was a musical or regular straight episode, the usual challenges applied from the production standpoint. Since the actors would be singing and dancing and not just walking, talking, and fighting, some accommodations had to be made in the area of the physical look of the episodes, while other areas went entirely unaffected.

Production Designer, **Carey Meyer**, talks about his early planning for the episode. "I experienced some trepidation about it because I had never worked on a musical. I was a little intimidated about the thought of doing the musical. So I went through a lot of research on musicals by starting to look at things and compare them to how our existing sets might lend themselves to the show and what I might need to come up with."

However, he soon found that his concerns were premature. Once he actually had the chance to sit down with the script, he discovered that demands for his designs would be minimal. "Joss wrote the musical almost entirely to existing sets," he explains. "Because of the complicated nature of the musical, he wanted to know the space intimately before we needed to get into preproduction. The end result really showed off our sets but made it much easier for me to deal with."

That's not to say that there wasn't anything new in the episode. A large portion of script, and especially the finale, took place in the Bronze. Carey was pleased to see the dance numbers used the entire set, which had been redesigned for season six. The numbers really had the chance to show off the new design even though it had not been specifically changed for that episode. However, he explains that one bit was added for the musical. "We did alter one part of the Bronze, which was the only thing we really had to build for the musical. We created the staircase that the demon dances down. The under-lit disks were designed specifically for that tap dancing number."

Like traditional episodes of *Buffy*, the action in this episode was not kept solely to the confines of the sets. There were several exteriors, including street scenes as well as dance numbers in a park and a cemetery. Carey explains how the episode gave them a chance to shoot at a location rarely used for filming. "We shot at a cemetery that we have typically never shot at before, because it's underneath

the flight path of LAX airport. Since it was a musical, there was no dialogue that needed to be recorded in those scenes. It's a great-looking cemetery, but it's usually difficult to shoot in because of the sound."

Another focal point was the park used in Tara's song, "Under Your Spell." The setting provided the exact look that production wanted to obtain. Carey explains why the spot worked so well. "There were a lot of natural elements in the park. There was a lake, a stream, and a nice little bridge. It was just sort of an idyllic place. But it wasn't too large that it took you out of the scene. It was just the right size and scope for what the scene called for and fit the needs perfectly."

Although he experienced initial concerns with doing the musical, Carey remembers the entire experience fondly. "Working on the musical was fantastic. And working with Joss in that format was a really great thing. The best thing for me was that because it was a musical it was an even more visual format and because we shot widescreen. The sets were just so much more grand to me."

The musical aspect of the episode did, however, affect some parts of the makeup design, acknowledges Makeup Supervisor, **Todd McIntosh**. "We were all expecting this episode to be something special, so we put in an extra effort. All of the beauty makeup, for example, was polished up a little bit more. When I do makeup, personally I see a difference between a drama series and comedy series and fantasy. On *Buffy* we have always had beauty makeup that was a little bit of a combination of the three. All of the girls look great all the time as much as we can for saving the reality. We pushed that a little further for the musical episode."

Todd goes on to explain one specific change. "With Emma, her makeup as a character is always a little retro. When we designed her makeup for that episode, we were specifically targeting that thirties style that her song came in, so her makeup was specifically designed to reflect the 1930s. I don't think that there were any other stylistic changes. When Spike morphs into the vampire, it was his regular makeup, but when he was in his regular straight makeup, we made sure he was extremely polished. And that's sort of the approach we took with everyone."

Beyond the beauty makeup of the cast, Todd is also responsible for overseeing the application of the special effects makeup and has a hand in the design aspect of those areas as well. Most of the demon designs are created by outside special effects makeup houses. But, no matter who designs the look, Todd confirms that like every other aspect of the episode it all comes from one creative idea. "Joss himself is the ultimate

force of all of those designs. It's his say and his vision. When he says, 'I want wooden puppet characters,' those drawings get done and they go back to him and then back and forth." And Joss was involved with overseeing all stages of design and sculpting for the episode.

For "Once More, With Feeling," it turns out there was a new design studio in the mix. **Joel Harlow** of Harlow FX had been brought onto the series beginning with episode six and continued working on the show through episode seventeen. Joel and his team created many of the memorable demons throughout the season, including the intricately designed loan shark in the episode that followed, "Tabula Rasa."

With the musical as the first show Joel was working on, he explains his need to impress. "Naturally we wanted to make a design statement and a quality statement with the work we generated for the episode. But we were also inspired by the fact that the musical was such an interesting idea. Both my partner, **Rob Henderstein**, and I always want to make the stuff that we put out to be something special."

Joel goes on to detail the process. "The first thing that I got was just a few pages of the story. There weren't many specific designs for the characters. Joss knew what he wanted, but we still had to do designs and go back and forth on ideas until we could show him what he was thinking." Joel and his team were responsible for the look of the singing demon in the opening number, the burning body that falls to Sweet's feet, and the freakishly scary puppet henchmen.

BUFFY THE VAMPIRE SLAYER
"ONCE MORE, WITH FEELING"
#6ABB07

Minion Design #3

One of Joel's favorite demons was the unnamed "Goat Demon" who performed in the opening of the show. Aside from the fact that he thought it was a great design, the entire look had been his vision, since the script only called for a cemetery demon. "When we got the job to start doing the special effects makeup, I just started designing random demons," Joel recalls. "That design was just a generic demon design. In my first meeting with Joss I threw it down on the table and he liked it and plugged it into that spot."

As much as the Goat Demon was an easy choice, the designs for Sweet's henchmen required considerably more work. "We really put a lot of work into the minions," Joel recalls. "They were initially mechanical heads with blinking and arching eyes, and all their mouths worked. In the episode we only see one of them with the mouth opening and closing. I think Joss's idea behind that was that he didn't want to make people think that they were singing, but they were fully articulated dummies. They could have done a lot more, but obviously understanding the place that they fit in the story, it made sense why they didn't."

Joel goes on to explain the uneasy feel generated by the puppetlike design. "The henchmen go back to that whole fear of clowns. I did a bunch of designs for that one—like five or six—and they were all sort of overtly frightening. One of them had nails coming out of his head like nails had been pounded into this wooden head. I think ultimately the one that Joss chose was more typical of a mannequin but still had hints of evil to it. I think that made it work a lot better. It was almost sort of the benign force at that point rather than something that jumps out and says *monster*."

Being only one part of the production team, Joel explains how the entire look of the character affects the makeup design. "There's certainly a lot of crossover with the costumer, **Cynthia Bergstrom**. Most of the demons that we had done for the series had to work in conjunction with the wardrobe because we had to hide things under clothing. We had to know what the wardrobe was to know how much of the creature we had to build and what we were going to see of it. As far as the look of the wardrobe, they pretty much came up with that and we floated around our designs so they knew the direction we were going."

Another challenge for the episode was the demon central to the plot. Sweet proved an especially difficult design for the team because Joss wanted a very specific look. Todd explains, "Joss had an image in his head that neither myself, Joel, nor any of the office staff were able to put on paper. The design was entirely **Robert Hall**. He went to Rob because he felt that Rob could interpret what he was trying to do."

Rob Hall and the team at Almost Human special makeup effects studios had never worked on *Buffy* before, but they had taken over the responsibility of makeup design for *Angel* that same season and, like *Buffy*, were already six episodes into production. Rob was responsible for many of the demons on the third season of *Angel*, including the affable Skip, who served as a guide helping Cordelia with her growing powers.

Rob jumped at the chance to work on the episode. "From the moment that I heard Joss was doing a musical, I thought that it was a brilliant idea. When he approached me about doing Sweet, I knew that it couldn't be just another demon. I knew that it couldn't be something like they had before, design-wise. Joss had this look in his eye when he talked about him. He told me that it was a big important character that had to be suave

"WALK THROUGH THE FIRE"
"The Red Shoes"

The concept of the "dancing demon" Sweet is unique to the episode "Once More, With Feeling." When summoned the demon comes to town and compels the townsfolk to communicate through song and dance, often admitting to their secret emotions as they do. The price he is paid is in taking the one who summoned him as a bride. However, the people affected by the spell that cannot stop singing and dancing pay the ultimate price when their excess energy causes them to burst into flames.

The premise of being afflicted by nonstop dancing is common in theatrical mythology and grows out of a children's story by Hans Christian Andersen called "The Red Shoes." The famous tale has been adapted into a ballet, which was further adapted into a classic 1948 film. Though Joss Whedon was familiar with the basic tale of a girl who cannot stop dancing he had not seen the famous movie or read the actual story prior to the filming of the episode. However, he did make a reference to it in the script.

A man is dancing, a frenetic little tap dance that he clearly has been doing for hours — he is sweaty and panicking, but, Red Shoe-like (the ballet not the diaries), he can't stop.

The original tale by Hans Christian Andersen revolves around a young girl who is punished when she insists upon wearing her red shoes to church repeatedly. The shoes are cursed with a spell so she must dance uncontrollably whenever she wears them. Though she is given the opportunity to put the shoes safely away, she cannot resist the temptation to wear them once more to a grand ball. This time, however, the shoes stick fast to her feet and she is forced to dance day and night as she travels across the countryside. Suffering from exhaustion and pain, she visits the executioner and has her feet cut off so she can begin to repent for her sin of vanity.

Excerpt from Hans Christian Andersen's original tale:

She danced out into the open churchyard, but the dead did not join her dance; they had something much better to do. She wanted to sit down on a pauper's grave where the bitter wormwood grew, but there was no rest nor repose for her. When she danced towards the open church door, she saw an angel standing there in long white robes and wings which reached from his shoulders to the ground. His face was grave and stern, and in his hand he held a broad and shining sword.

"Dance you shall!" said he. "You shall dance in your red shoes till you are pale and cold. Till your skin shrivels up and you are a skeleton! You shall dance from door to door, and wherever you find proud vain children, you must knock at the door so that they may see you and fear you. Yes, you shall, dance—!"

Bibliography

Fairy Tales of Hans Christian Andersen. The Orion Press / New York. Distributed by Crown Publishers, Inc. From the edition published by arrangement with Giulio Einaudi Editore-Torino

and slick. He couldn't just look like a guy or a demon. He had to have an inner thing. I got what he was talking about." Even though Rob had a good idea of the direction he was going to pursue, he still had a challenge ahead of him with only three days to design and create the prosthetic makeup.

Rob immediately set to work on the designs for Sweet. "We did a lot of interesting things with his features," he explains. "He's very asymmetrical. He's got a thing on his chin that's almost very musical, like a musical note." Coming late into the process, Rob also had the opportunity to work with the existing elements. "We saw the costume the actor was going to be wearing and saw how snazzy it was. Between the outfit and talking to Joss, I got the idea to give him an iridescent feel to his paint job. His overall skin tone is iridescent, much like the silk suit that he wears."

The inspiration, however, did not stop there. As Rob explains, "He also wears the jewel in his forehead that Dawn had in the amulet—that was Joss's idea. I had the idea to give him the nose ring and earrings. There were cool little hints like that. He's actually got some gold fingernails on his pinky—just little hints of things. Overall he's a demon and a bad guy, but he's got style."

Once again the design process hit some potential snags with the musical portion of the episode. Rob recalls that his first concern was with the heavy amount of dancing the actor was required to do while in makeup. "From the moment we got the call, everyone was pretty worried that the actor, **Hinton Battle**, would sweat the makeup off. Of course I was horrified so I put on layers and layers of glue. I realized after the first day that it was a bit of 'crying wolf.' He didn't sweat that badly. But it was certainly something to take into consideration that someone would get hot from dancing. I mean, you're certainly hot enough when you're wearing prosthetics. When you're wearing a suit and you're indoors dancing and singing, there's a whole lot that comes into play."

Dancing was not the only problem, since Sweet did have some singing, or at least lip-syncing to his pre-recorded tracks, as well. Rob notes that this did affect his work slightly. "When I was applying the makeup, it was especially important around the mouth. I had to make sure the makeup was a little more secure around the mouth than I normally would for just a guy who's just running out and going 'grrrr arrgh.'"

Overall, Rob was happy with the finished product. "I thought that the lighting staff had done an amazing job lighting him, because you could really see the iridescence of the paint, which is what I had hoped. There were a lot of really nice light fills on his face. He had a lot of nice close-ups so you could really see all the detail in his eyes and the cool contact lenses we had put on him. I thought he turned out pretty nice."

Like the makeup, Cynthia Bergstrom's costumes also played an integral role in the musical. Aside from the normal everyday wardrobe worn by the actors, several of the outfits were chosen specifically for their musical flair. But, whether the costume was used in a large production number or a simpler scene, Cynthia had an overall plan. "Throughout the episode there was a very subtle color coding going on. I had picked various colors for each character. Alyson's colors were different hues of purple. When she got to the musical number in the park, I put her in a dress that was more pink and soft to romanticize the undertones of love. It needed to look modern, but it also needed to look a step out of place. I think that the whole beauty of musicals from past eras is that everything was a little bit romanticized."

In keeping with past eras, Xander and Anya's pajamas were a total retro look reminiscent of the Noel Coward bedroom comedies of the thirties and forties. As with other elements pertaining to "I'll Never Tell," this look was also built around Anya. Cynthia explains, "Emma has always reminded me of Carole Lombard. Throughout the seasons, I've based her costume choices on a zany, wacky, Girl Friday look. In that number, I just thought it would be cute and quirky to give them more of a forties feel. Also, in talking with Joss, costume-wise, he felt that he had a forties swing vibe going on, which spurred on my imagination as well."

Cynthia's work naturally spilled over to the guest characters like Sweet's forties-style zoot suit that changes from bold red to blue with the snap of a finger. But, unlike traditional episodes, the costumer also found herself choosing outfits for the extras. Since most of the background dancers were playing specific roles, Cynthia also had the task of choosing their looks, right down to the rainbow of outfits held aloft during the ode to dry cleaning.

It was the responsibility of the director of photography, **Ray Stella**, to literally show the designs in the best light. However, he also had the additional task of doing it all while filming for a widescreen. Ray had worked in film before and was quite familiar with the format, and actually prefers it to the regular televison screen because of its grandeur. "It's a little more work," he admits, "and a little bit more to light, because you can't just let that stuff fall off on the edges. So it takes a little more time. Other than that, I just prefer it."

Although *Angel* had already been filming in widescreen, this was the only episode of *Buffy* to date that had used that format. Joss explains why the choice was natural. "I actually studied film musicals in college and beside being a stage musical nut, I adore the old musicals *The Bandwagon*, *Singin' in the Rain*, and the big widescreen ones, particularly *Brigadoon*, *Les Girls*, and that era in the fifties when everything got really wide. I knew this episode had to be widescreen. It was going to be a musical, so no matter what it had to be wide. Like I said, I don't like to do formal tricks for their own sake, but there is a different experience viewing something in that shape that I wanted to capture. It just felt right."

The fact that the episode was a musical did not really affect the lighting since the show already has a fantasy element to it. However, Ray does note that he did make some special considerations for the lighting. "In some instances I made it a little more broad. For instance in the Xander/Anya sequence in the apartment I had some pretty broad stroke lighting coming through the windows. Other than that, the lighting was pretty much the same as what I do. I keep the dark parts dark enough to be spooky but light enough to see the faces."

There were some challenges that had nothing to do with the special nature of the episode. Ray recalls that the one challenge he had was simply a result of an extravagant location shoot. "The cemetery scene at night with the demons and Sarah required a lot of light because we showed a lot of the cemetery. In those situations, it takes time, and matching the moment-to-moment shots can be a little tricky if you're not careful. Being an all-nighter made it a little bit difficult too, but it was nothing we don't do all the time."

Overall, Ray was pleased with the entire experience. "I always enjoy working with Joss. This is my second episode I shot for him as the director." Ray was also Director of Photography on "The Body." "Joss has got a great vision and he knows exactly what he wants. He's very specific and knows when he has the shot. He sets up some really nice stuff. It's fun being around him."

"Something to sing about"

As the script notes, "Once More, With Feeling" opens with an orchestral version of the familiar *Buffy the Vampire Slayer* theme with classic-style movie musical opening credits. The action of the story begins with a typical overture comprised of selections from the songs to be performed throughout the episode. The score is played under the action of a typical day in Sunnydale.

The opening number, "Going Through the Motions," has the responsibility of setting the tone for the musical. Right at the start it needs to bring the audience seamlessly into the unique episode. Conveniently, it was the one number that Joss Whedon had the clearest image of the start. "'Going Through the Motions' was a pure Disney number. It was what Jeffrey Katzenberg calls the 'I want,' which is where the heroine explains her problems like the song 'Part of Your World' in *The Little Mermaid*."

With the motivation behind the number set, he had no problem blocking out the scene. "By the time I shot it," he explains, "I already had every visual worked out perfectly in my head. I knew I wanted that last big powerful note to be like in 'Part of Your World,' where Ariel's face comes out from behind her hair. When Buffy sang the last note, I wanted her face to appear from behind a dusting vampire. It's both amusing and very emotional. Sarah never looked better. And then I knew I wanted to do the big pull back with the gently blowing vampire dust swirling into frame. Stuff like that was easy."

The scene in the Magic Box establishes that this is indeed a traditional musical theater construct with dialogue interspersed throughout as opposed to the pop operas of more recent years in which all dialogue is sung. The straight scene then leads into "I Have a Theory," which is a traditional multipart piece for the cast with an explosive pop song dropped in. Joss explains the origin of Anya's rock lament over the bunnies. "In 'Fear, Itself,' Xander told Anya to wear something scary for Halloween and she wore a big bunny outfit. From there it became a running gag. Now, Emma herself occasionally breaks into heavy metal screaming for no reason. She'd just do this on the stage sometimes to crack me up. So I knew I was going

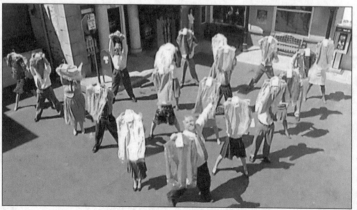

to write her a little heavy metal rock opera moment and I thought what better thing to sing about than the horror of bunnies."

Following this number, the gang and the audience learn that it is not just the Scoobies that are affected by the musical malady. This is done when Buffy pops her head outside to witness the completion of a rousing production number in honor of the fine abilities of the dry cleaner. The lead singer in this number, simply referred to as "Man" in the script, is none other than Coexecutive Producer David Fury.

David had a background in musical theater having performed in *The Fantasticks* for a year in New York, as well as *Kiss Me Kate, Cabaret*, and numerous other shows and regional theater musicals. David recalls how he got into the episode. "Back when Joss was talking about doing a musical episode, I reminded him of my past as a musical comedy performer and said, 'If there's any opportunity for me to do something in the musical, I would love to do it.' And he said, 'Absolutely. There'll be room for everyone.' When Joss delivered it and we heard the music I thought it was the best score I've heard in years. And suddenly I was not just pleased to be in it, I was honored."

The action continues leading into the naughtily romantic song "Under Your Spell," as performed by Amber Benson to an impressed production crew. "Amber was particularly great," David recalls. "I knew she could sing. I didn't know how well she could sing, but Joss did. He gave her the most demanding ballad in the episode."

Chris Beck agrees with David's assessment of Amber, adding that the entire number worked for a variety of reasons. "I like 'Under Your Spell' best because it's a great song and it was sung really well. I feel it's

a great combination of what both Jesse and I had to offer. There's always one song that, for whatever the reason, the planets align and production, arrangement, writing--everything just happens. I think it happened on that one. I think it's the best written song in the show and I also think it's the best sounding song in the show from a production perspective."

Sweet's introduction is brief and menacing. The unknown demon in brightly colored garb watches as a dancing man burns up at his feet. This quickly introduces the threat of the episode and that all the song and dance belies a sinister purpose.

The following morning, Xander and Anya wake up wearing very retro looking pajamas and immediately break into one of the classic numbers of the musical. Joss details how this particular number grew directly from the characters. "I knew that I wanted a whole retro thing for Xander and Anya because Anya has that feel to her and their apartment also has that feel. I knew visually it would just be right for them. And they were sort of the comic couple. Everything was tailored to what already existed."

After they collapse on the couch laughing, Xander and Anya express their frustration over this musical dilemma to Giles. In a street scene on the move, Giles details the facts he has learned about the dancing demon, providing exposition for the audience. The scene has an additional function of showing tidbits of how the entire town is affected by the singing and dancing.

In a second production cameo, Coexecutive Producer Marti Noxon pops up trying to sing her way out of a parking ticket. The self-proclaimed musical-theater geek explains how she came to appear. "When David Fury made it known that he would love a cameo, I was like, 'Me too! Put me in! Put me in!' Then Joss did and I was like, 'Take me out! Take me out!' I hadn't really thought it through. I was just talking the talk and the next thing I knew he had written this little part. I got a total case of cold feet and wanted out, but he wouldn't let me. And then it ended up being a tremendous amount of fun and very, very self-indulgent. I wouldn't do it again. But as a one time experience, it was wonderful."

With two of the production staff making brief appearances, it sort of begs the question of why Joss Whedon himself did not appear in the musical. He did pop up once in an episode of *Angel* in which, under heavy makeup, he played Numfar, the frenetically dancing member of Lorne's family. However, he was considerably reluctant to make a more notable cameo in this episode. "Let's just say the stuff that I wrote wasn't exactly for my voice," he notes. "You don't really want to be self-indulgent. I needed those pieces to show what was happening in the world and I knew Marti had a beautiful voice. I also knew David was a performer and could sing, so it just made sense to put them in. But I wasn't going to write a little vanity thing for myself. That would be lame."

Much like the retro aspect of "I'll Never Tell" grew out of Anya's characterization, the more heavy rocking tune "Rest In Peace" was a purely Spike number. David Fury recalls the unique setting for that number. "Being out in the cemetery in the middle of the night with James Marsters and Sarah, shooting them doing 'Rest in Peace' was kind of beautiful and surreal. We were in a real graveyard. And seeing James just cut loose in this great rock-and-roll song was really spectacular. I knew right there how special this was going to be because it was one of the most exciting musical moments I've seen on film."

Jesse Tobias also comments on the power of the number. "James really surprised me. He was really committed to a good performance. I had a good idea from talking with Joss about what he wanted for that song, stylistically and musically. I talked to James about it and he really stepped up to the plate. I thought it was a really emotional performance."

Following the revelation that Willow put Tara under a spell, Dawn is kidnapped by Sweet's puppet henchmen. When she awakens on the pool table, her ballet-like dance number begins, which evolves into Sweet's jazzier tap dance. Using the redesigned Bronze set, Ray Stella lit the place for maximum effect. "I enjoyed the Bronze part of the musical

the best, where Sweet is dancing with Michelle and later Sarah does her dance. In the Bronze there's a truss of lighting that is above the dance floor. I tried to create pools of light so as they moved through the dance floor they would go in and out of different lights. In the background I projected colored light onto the actors to give it a more theatrical look and make it look more like a musical dance number on a stage. I achieved more of the theatrical look through the use of primary colors."

Joss notes that the success of Sweet's number came from a couple of sources. First and foremost was Adam Shankman's choreography. As Adam explains the work with Sweet, "My motivation was simply looking at who the character was as well as the actor portraying him. I then listened to the music and I knew what the space was that we were in. Then I listened to the lyrics and Joss told me what he needed in terms of the message that needed to be conveyed. His music dictated what I did in the framework of the piece."

Joss explains that the success of this number was also a result of postproduction. "I didn't really get a chance to work the choreography because things got kind of rushed. I put Hinton on a proscenium and pretty much watched him and then said, 'Put the cameras here and here and here.' That was more like regular television directing. It was just sort of figure it out when it's in front of you and then cut it together the best way you can. My editor, **Lisa Lassek**, did a great job on that scene. I hardly changed a frame of her original cut. She did a lot of cutting and in a way it's kind of Fosse-like in that respect."

Meanwhile, Joss was much more comfortable on the directing of "Standing in Your Way," the ballad performed in which Giles reveals his hidden feelings. "I prefer the numbers that I really understood, like Tony's number was the slow motion piece that I had mapped out before we did it. The ones that are very controlled are fun to make when you're doing the number because you know exactly what the next step is."

"Under Your Spell"
Lethe's Bramble

Ingredient used in the spell Willow cast to cause Tara to forget their fight over the abuse of magic

"Lethe" is taken from Greek Mythology. It is the name of one of the five rivers of Hades that serve as a boundary between the lands of the living and the dead. The river, which flows through the plain of Lethe, consists of waters that when drunk by the souls of the dead cause them to forget their former lives. Aptly called "the river of forgetfulness" and "the river of oblivion," it flows through the cave of Hypnos, the god of sleep, where it induced drowsiness. The other four rivers of Hades are the Acheron, the Kokytos, the Phlegethon, and, most notably, the Styx.

The word "lethe" means loss of memory and is the root for the word "lethargy," meaning drowsiness or inactivity.

"Bramble" is the familiar name for a species of prickly plants or shrubs in the rose family.

The powerful reprise to "Under Your Spell" follows Tara's confirmation that Willow had placed a spell on her. The number evolves into a duet with Giles in which he and Tara both say they wish they could stay. Marti Noxon explains the significance of this turning point. "The show takes a shift in the third act when you suddenly realize that it's not just going to be this light-hearted romp. It takes some very pivotal character shifts and moves the story forward and leaves the characters in very different places than they were before. All of a sudden you realize, 'Oh, my God, this is actually going to change everything. It's not only a musical, it's a musical with a point.'"

Sweet's henchman enters the Magic Box and reveals the location of the demon and the fact that he has Buffy's sister. Giles first tells Buffy to perform the rescue on her own before he accepts the fact that she still needs the gang's help. The conflicting emotions of the moment lead to the dramatic "Walk Through the Fire," which was David Fury's personal favorite. "I think that was one of the most sophisticated numbers, musically and lyrically. Having all of the characters sing in it—obviously it was patterned after a sort of 'Tonight' number from *West Side Story*. I think it has enormous power, and it's incredibly catchy. It's just a very cool number."

And yet, with all of the amazing work put into the episode, Joss notes that it was just one seemingly simple moment that stood out for him. "Probably the greatest highlight of the entire experience was when that goddamned fire engine hit its mark on the right note every time we shot it. That was the most extraordinary thing. I still don't know how they arranged that."

The battle won—sort of—the gang gets together for one last song to ask the musical question, "Where do we go from here?" The final number sums up the experience and throws one last little revelation into the mix. "It's such a rich hour of television," Marti says. "So much happens. To me, the last scene in the Bronze where Buffy acknowledges that she was in Heaven to all of her friends and there's that feeling of disconnect that follows. Everybody thought they knew where they stood, and now everything's up in the air. And then the big kiss with Buffy and Spike at the end--that's what killed me."

However, if it had been a normal episode, it would have ended minutes before they even reached that climactic point. "It ran long," Joss notes with a tinge of regret, "for which I thank UPN and berate myself. I really didn't want it to run long. I was adamant that it would just be a regular old episode despite how much work it took. I just wrote too much and couldn't get it out."

With the current trend of Hollywood movies going on to Broadway, the question naturally arises about the Great White Way as a possible destination for *Buffy the Vampire Slayer*. While a retelling of "Once More, With Feeling" probably wouldn't work outside of the context of season six, the overall idea is not without merit, Joss admits. "The possibility of a stand-alone Broadway musical has been bandied about since year one of *Buffy*. Some people have offered to write it, but hey, if there's going to be a *Buffy* musical, I want to write it. Part of me thinks it would be really intriguing, while another part of me is like, 'For the love of God, can I write something that's not *Buffy*?'"

Joss is keeping busy with a number of projects beyond the scope of *Buffy*, but that series will clearly always be most dear to his heart. "Once More, With Feeling" is obviously one of Joss's personal highlights from the long running series. "It was so much incredible work. It was such a joy. Everybody worked harder than I'd ever seen. I was both aglow and exhausted the entire time. There are moments in the show that still really thrill me even while I cringe at everything I do. The big kiss between Sarah and James at the end. Michelle's little thing on the pool table when she wakes up was an image I had from the very start. Emma and Nick's dance number. Amber and Aly on the bridge, which I thought was a beautiful location. And Tony and Amber singing. Musically the Tony and Amber piece was my favorite. You don't get to do that every day."

Epilogue

"Where Do We Go from Here?"

The sad musical ended with the simple question of what would become of the group of friends now that their innermost feelings were revealed. Unfortunately the events that followed only served to worsen their predicaments.

Giles did return to England, leaving the Slayer on her own to fend with Dawn. The younger Summers sister continued her small rebellions—i.e., stealing—as the neglect worsened. Even Dawn's inadvertent summoning of a vengeance demon was not enough to make Buffy fully realize her sister's need to be accepted as a young adult. It would take a climactic battle to stave off yet another apocalypse for the sisters to work together as a team and for Buffy to see that her Dawn was indeed growing.

Xander and Anya continued to fret about their coming wedding. By the wedding day they had failed to allay their concerns, especially Xander. Afraid of embarking on a life like his parents', Xander walked out on his bride moments before the nuptials were to take place. In the weeks that followed, he could never truly explain his reason for abandoning her. In anger, Anya went back to her demon ways, but was unable to seek the vengeance she so desired because her love for Xander prevented her from doing so. But the pain lived on, and she sought comfort in a meaningless physical encounter with Spike.

But Anya was not the only one of the gang to turn to Spike for intimate relations. Following their orchestra-swelling kiss, Buffy and Spike cultivated a sexual relationship with an intensity that destroyed buildings. For Spike it was a true declaration of his feelings, but for Buffy, who believed that she had come back from Heaven "wrong," it was the only way she knew of to make herself feel something—and it was certainly not love. Buffy finally broke it off when she realized how she was only hurting herself and ultimately Spike as well. In a fit of anger, the vampire attacked her before leaving Sunnydale. The season finale saw the restoration of his soul, but it remains to be seen what influence said soul will have on the vamp's psyche.

It was for Willow that the revelations proved most devastating. Though Tara gave her the chance to forgo her magical ways, Willow discovered the need for power was too strong and tried to cast a mismanaged spell to make Buffy forget her time in Heaven. She and Tara fought, prompting yet another spell—this one with the intention of causing Tara to forget the argument. When all was revealed, Tara left her girlfriend, sending Willow in a spiral of depression that turned into an addiction to magic. It was only when her problem grew so dangerous that Dawn was hurt that she and her other friends truly accepted the seriousness of the problem.

Willow's life seemed to get back on track as she recovered from her addiction. Tara returned, and the pair shared a romantic night that tragically ended with Tara's accidental death at the hands of Warren the following morning. In a fit of rage, Willow fully embraced the dark magicks and turned into a witch with inhu-

manly evil power. After seeking vengeance on the murderer, Willow's anger grew unchecked as she went after his accomplices and, ultimately, the rest of the world. In the end, it was Xander who came to her rescue. With a little help from healing magick provided by a returned Giles, Xander reintroduced his friend to the power of love. It took many months and much sadness, but the gang finally found a bittersweet "happy" ending.

Buffy the Vampire Slayer

"I just want to feel alive." —BUFFY

BUFFY: *"Last night, did anybody, oh . . . burst into song? . . . Like you were in a musical or something?"*

XANDER: *"Merciful Zeus."*

GILES: *". . . [of] course that would explain the huge backing orchestra."*

"Sweet"
OPTION 1

"Sweet"
OPTION 2

Sweet

"Now we're partying."
—SWEET

GILES: *"What does [Sweet] want?"*

HENCHMAN *(pointing to Buffy)*: *"Her. Plus chaos and insanity and people burning up, but that's more big picture stuff."*

"So Dawn's in trouble. It must be Tuesday."
—BUFFY

REVELATIONS AND DECISIONS

"So one by one they come to me . . . but what they'll find ain't what they have in mind." —SWEET

"Give me something to sing about." —BUFFY

THE END

A 20TH CENTURY FOX TELEVISION PRODUCTION

Sheet Music

OVERTURE/GOING THROUGH THE MOTIONS

Words and Music by
JOSS WHEDON

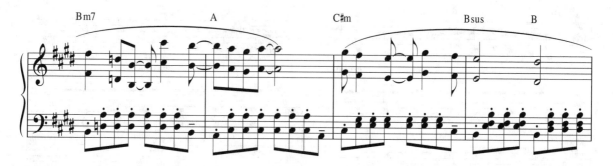

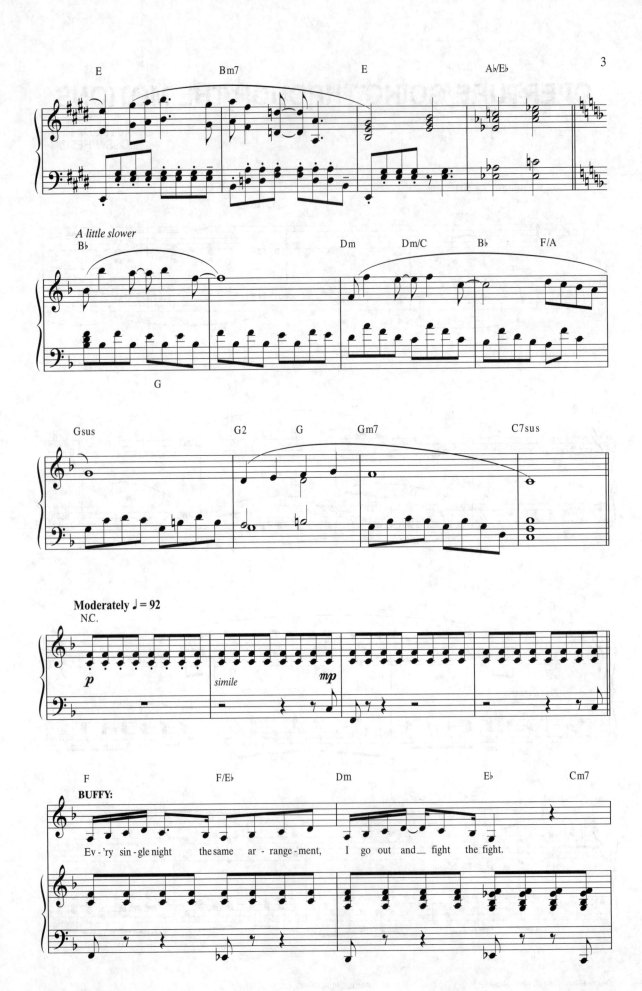

4

Still, I al-ways feel this strange es - trange - ment, noth-ing here is real, noth-ing here is right.

I've been mak-ing shows of trad - ing blows, just hop - ing no one knows that I've been

go - ing through the mo - tions,___ walk - ing through the part.___

Noth-ing seems_ to pen - e - trate my_____ heart.___

6

I'VE GOT A THEORY/BUNNIES/WE'RE TOGETHER

Words and Music by
JOSS WHEDON

4

witch - es, they were per - se - cut - ed, wic - ca good and love the earth and

E   F#m   E/G#   A   N.C.

ANYA:

wom - an pow'r and I'll be o - ver here.   I've got a theo - ry,

G   N.C.

it could be bun - nies.

A   N.C.

TARA:

I've got a...

D   E   B

ANYA:

Bun - nies aren't just cute like ev - 'ry - bod - y sup - pos -

6

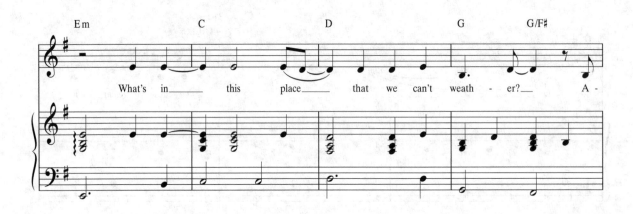

8

Em   C   D   G   G/F#

GROUP:

What can't___ we do___ if we get in it?

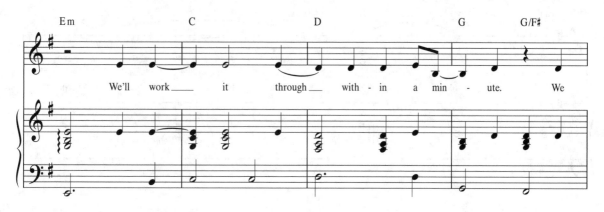

Em   C   D   G   G/F#

We'll work___ it through___ with - in a min - ute. We

Bm   Am

have to try,___ we'll pay the price,_____ it's

Bm   **BUFFY:**   A

do or die.___ Hey, I've died twice!___

9

UNDER YOUR SPELL

Words and Music by
JOSS WHEDON

Verse:

TARA:

1. I lived my life in shadow, never the sun on my
2. I saw a world enchanted, spirits and charms in the

face. It didn't seem so sad, though,
air. I always took for grant - ed

3

I'LL NEVER TELL

Words and Music by
JOSS WHEDON

Moderately bright (♩ = 132)

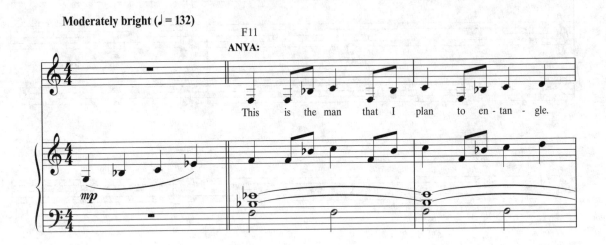

4

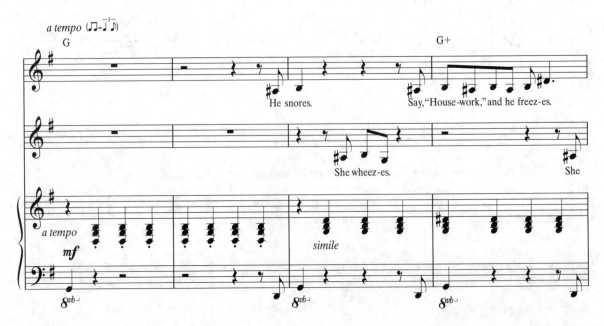

6

His eyes are bead-y.

clings, she's need-y. She's al-so real-ly greed-y. She nev-er...   This is my verse. Hel-lo.

8

You know_____ my knight in

You know_____ you're quite the charm - er.

ar - mor.

You're the cut - est of the scoo - bies with your lips as red as ru - bies. And your

firm yet sup - ple tight em - brace.

10

lied,_____ I said it's eas - y._____ I've__ tried_____

lied,_____ I said it's eas - y._____ I've__ tried_____

__ but there's__ these fears I can't quell.____

__ but there's__ these fears I can't quell.____ Is she look - ing__ for a

Will I look good when__ I've got - ten old?

pot of gold? Will our

12

REST IN PEACE

Words and Music by
JOSS WHEDON

Moderate rock ♩ = 88

SPIKE:
Verses 1, 2 & 3:

1. I died so man-y years a - go, but
2. 3. *See additional lyrics*

you can make me feel like it is - n't so. But

why you come to be with me, I think I fi - n'lly know,

4

6

but I fol - low you like a man

pos - sessed. There's a trai - tor here be - neath

my breast, and it hurts me more than you've ev -

cresc. poco a poco

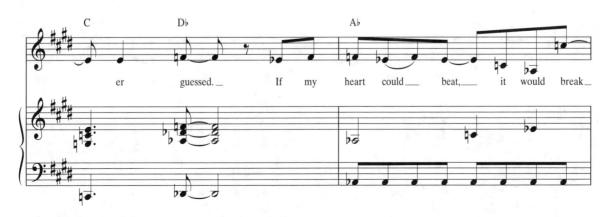

er guessed. If my heart could beat, it would break

7

8

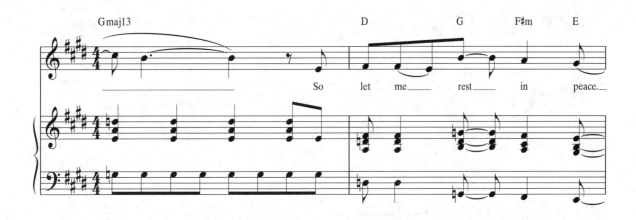

Verse 2:
You're scared,
Ashamed of what you feel.
And you can't tell the ones you love;
You know they couldn't deal.
But whisper in a dead man's ear,
That doesn't make it real.

Verse 3:
That's great,
But I don't wanna play.
'Cause being with you touches me
More than I can say.
And since I'm only dead to you,
I'm sayin' stay away
And let me rest in peace.
(To Chorus:)

WHAT YOU FEEL

Words and Music by
JOSS WHEDON

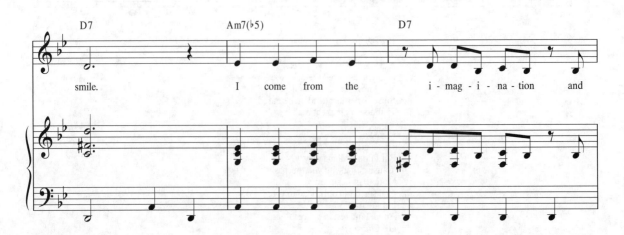

3

4

6

Ab   Gm   F   D7

back we will go to my king-dom be-low____ and you will be my queen.____

Gm   Cm7   **DAWN:**   D7

No, you see you and me would-n't

DEMON:

'Cause I know what__ you feel,____ girl.__

Gm7   Cm7

be ver - y re - gal.   What I

I'll_____ make it real,

8

STANDING

Words and Music by
JOSS WHEDON

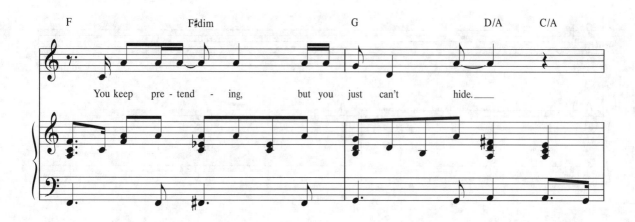

Standing - 5 - 1

4

6

UNDER YOUR SPELL/STANDING - REPRISE

Words and Music by
JOSS WHEDON

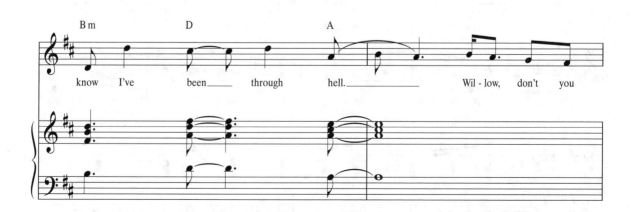

4

5

WALK THROUGH THE FIRE

Words and Music by
JOSS WHEDON

6

SOMETHING TO SING ABOUT

Words and Music by
JOSS WHEDON

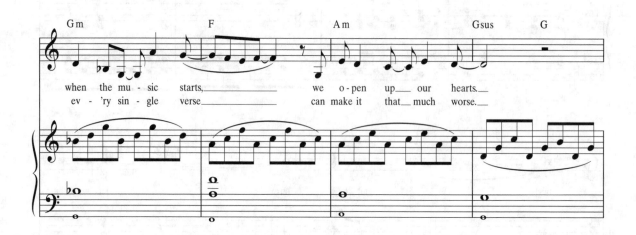

3

6

WHERE DO WE GO FROM HERE?

Words and Music by
JOSS WHEDON

Where Do We Go From Here? - 4 - 1

4

fear.___ Tell me,___ where do we go___ from___

___ here?_____ When does "The End"___ ap -

pear? When do the trum - pets

cheer?_____ The cur - tains close on a kiss, God knows, we can

Into every generation a Slayer is born...

Buffy the vampire slayer™
roleplaying game

NOW YOU CAN BECOME
PART OF THE SLAYER'S WORLD

Want to know more?

www.BTVSrpg.com

Everyone's got his demons....

ANGEL™

If it takes an eternity, he will make amends.

Original stories based
on the TV show
Created by Joss Whedon
& David Greenwalt

Available from Simon Pulse
Published by Simon & Schuster

2311-01

. . . A GIRL BORN
WITHOUT THE FEAR GENE

FEARLESS™

A SERIES BY
FRANCINE PASCAL

PUBLISHED BY SIMON & SCHUSTER

3029-01

ROSWELL™

ALIENATION DOESN'T END WITH GRADUATION

Everything changed the day Liz Parker died. Max Evans healed her, revealing his alien identity. But Max wasn't the only "Czechoslovakian" to crash down in Roswell. Before long Liz, her best friend Maria, and her ex-boyfriend Kyle are drawn into Max, his sister Isabel, and their friend Michael's life-threatening destiny.

Now high school is over, and the group has decided to leave Roswell to turn that destiny around. The six friends know they have changed history by leaving their home.

What they don't know is what lies in store…

SIMON PULSE
Published by Simon & Schuster